FRANCES ELLEN

A Threat To Remain

First published by Wolfkin BV 2021

Cover design by Arjuna Jay, https://arjunajayofficial.artstation.com. Elements of the cover design, and the chapter separators, have been taken from Freepik.com.

First edition

ISBN: 9789083086859

This book was professionally typeset on Reedsy. Find out more at reedsy.com

Contents

Dedication

For Timothy,

My best friend from back in English class, and best friend still. How our knowledge of the English language has improved since then. I love reading your feedback on early versions of my stories. How you invest with such enthusiasm gives me more energy to write than you will ever know.

Chapter 1

It had been in the early hours, long before sunrise, that Axel Reed started his shift of monitoring the Asters during their mission in North America. By the light of a single lamp on the corner desk in the Board Room, Axel had taken Sylvia's place and had settled into the desk chair.

The Asters had been in North America for a couple of days, but Axel hadn't received any updates yet. That wasn't unusual. They had their orders, and they were to follow them by any means necessary. They didn't need to check in every few hours with whoever was on watch. Jackson Kelly had trained them well. Axel Reed trusted their judgment and knew they would call for help if they needed it.

Axel kept an eye on the screen hanging above the desk. The screen showed five separate portrait images of each of the Asters. The monitors were fed signals from the transmission chips that all the Asters wore in their upper right arm, that sent back information on their whereabouts and their physical health. As long as their images were all shining brightly, Axel knew all five of them were fine.

Hours went by without any of the images changing. Axel turned on both computers in front of him. On the right-hand screen he opened up a live map of Brazil, specifically, the area where Diallo, the Ceder of Strength, and his investigation team were. One blue dot represented Diallo. There were no black dots anywhere in his area, meaning that he and his team were at no risk from a Disciple attack.

On the left-hand screen he opened up the physical health images of the four remaining Ceders. Rose, Katherine and all the Affinites from the Bone Recovery mission had returned to Saluverus already. Only Diallo's team was still in Brazil. Madeleine would shimmer them back in two days' time.

And then everything from South America would be closed off. Axel thought it was time. The Queen's Search teams hadn't definitively found out how far Gayle had run before she was killed, but the risks of staying in the Amazon longer to find out highly outweighed the benefits at this point. With ten Affinites ambushed and killed, and Percy Kelly still in a critical condition, the investigation into Gayle's death had been a complete disaster. Not to mention that the search for Cara and Tomas' bones had turned out to be nothing more than a wild goose chase, set up by the new South American King, probably for his own amusement.

That no Affinite of the Bone Recovery team had gone missing or had been killed, was probably only due to the fact that there were two Ceders present. The same went for why Eva Kelly's search team was attacked and not Diallo's.

Even so, Axel wanted to keep an eye on Diallo's surroundings just in case. He wanted no more casualties in South America. They needed to draw a line under this chapter, and look to the future.

Through the window, Axel saw the sun starting to rise over Saluverus. He glanced at the clock and realised Nicholas Nelson would soon come in for his shift.

There was a knock on the door.

"Come in," Axel called.

The door opened and Sylvia Allen, the island's Consul, stepped inside. She was carrying a large book under her arm. Her eyes immediately went to the screen above the corner desk. Axel would have done the same; first check if the Asters were still all right, then focus on the reason for coming.

"What is it?" Axel asked, expecting Nicholas, not Sylvia.

Sylvia tore her eyes away from the screen and looked at the Ambassador. "The speech therapist has arrived for Percy Kelly," she said, speaking lightly, and taking no offense at Axel's hard tone.

"And he is the best?" Axel asked.

Sylvia inclined her head. "He is exactly who Olga Masalis wanted. If anyone knows how to get Percy to speak normally and tell us what happened in the Amazon, it's him."

Axel thought of the gibberish that Percy Kelly spoke the last time the Ambassador visited him. The ex-soldier hadn't formed a single, comprehensible sentence since his return from the Amazon Rainforest. Even though Axel was calling back all the investigative teams, he still wanted to know what had happened there, so the Asters might be more prepared if they were ever to face the South American King and his Disciples again.

"He'd better manage to," Axel said. He glanced at the computer screens on the desk. "I've still got one team in the Amazon with no idea of what they could possibly face."

"They have Diallo with them. No Disciples would be stupid enough to launch an attack with him there. Not even the more dangerous and rogue ones," Sylvia said.

"If he says *anything* about what happened out there, you tell me immediately," Axel ground out, ignoring Sylvia's attempt to reassure him.

It was as good as a dismissal. Axel wasn't in the right headspace to ask any further questions about the genius therapist, who was supposed to help Percy Kelly regain his speech. They already had Olga Masalis on the case. If she felt the need to get help from a speech therapist, Axel wasn't going to question it. He needed Percy up and talking as soon as possible.

Though Axel thought their conversation had ended, Sylvia remained where she stood. Axel looked up at her. "What is it?" he asked her, not kindly.

Sylvia glanced at the book under her arm, which Axel now realised was not a book, but a large photo album. "You tasked us with finding out how the South American King discovered Gayle's location," she said.

Axel raised his eyebrows. "You found something?"

"Nothing concrete; it's just a hunch, but..." Sylvia walked over to where Axel was sitting, placed the album on the desk and flicked through the pages until she found the one she was looking for. "Do you remember her?"

Sylvia tapped her finger on a large picture showing three women. Axel recognised the middle woman immediately. "Aline Sosa," he said. "She was the Affinite who took care of Gayle when her parents weren't around."

Sylvia nodded. "As an extra layer of protection. Only five people knew the precise location of Gayle's hometown: you, Nicholas, Madeleine, Percy, and her. If the new King had tortured any of those first four to find out Gayle's location, we would have known."

Axel suddenly understood what Sylvia was getting at. "And we don't know about her, because she died when Gayle was fifteen."

"She was struck by lightning," Sylvia added.

Axel looked up at that. Lightning was Astaroth's power, and would be the new King's, as well. "Why didn't we take the necessary actions? Why didn't they move after this incident?"

"Because it was a freak accident," Sylvia said. "Or so it seemed at the time. Aline had come back from a four-day holiday. Cara and Tomas weren't around when she came to spend the afternoon with Gayle. She and Gayle went to a lake to swim when the storm hit. Gayle witnessed the whole thing."

Axel nodded slowly, the events of three years earlier coming back to him.

"We didn't think anything of it, because the lightning came from the sky. And if the King had been there in person to strike Aline, Gayle would have seen it. Plus, he would've gone after Gayle straight after, which didn't happen," Sylvia continued.

"So why is it suspect now?" Axel asked.

"Because in a statement Percy got from Gayle, she said that Aline was anxious that day when she came back, and claimed she had something very important to tell her parents when they returned. And under no circumstances did she want Gayle to go anywhere alone. What if those four days weren't a holiday? What if what she needed to tell Cara and Tomas was that she had been taken and forced or tricked into revealing her location? It could explain why the King only struck Aline, and didn't go after Gayle there and then. If he never intended to get Gayle that day, he didn't need to be present to strike with lightning. He could just control the storm from a distance and manipulate the lightning in a single strike."

Axel tapped his fingers on the desk as he thought. In reality, what Sylvia was saying was nothing more than speculation. The Small Council didn't think anything of Aline's unfortunate death at the time. Even Cara, Tomas and Percy thought it was just an accident and nothing more. Though the way Sylvia talked about it now... it did seem possible. Axel looked down at the picture of the Brazilian Affinite. Was Aline Sosa the reason they'd lost their Queen?

"Did we ever have any doubts about her when we hired her to look after Gayle?" Axel asked.

Sylvia shook her head. "Not a single one. That's why we hired her."

Axel closed his eyes and nodded. "See what more you can find out. As likely as this seems now, we need to make sure we're not spoiling an innocent woman's memory."

Sylvia bowed her head, took the album from the desk and left the room.

In the silence of the Board Room, Axel kept his eyes on the five images of the Asters. He tried to focus on them and not think about Aline Sosa and her possible betrayal. Axel tried not to think about how he remembered her *post mortem* showed only signs of electrocution, and nothing that hinted at abuse or torture.

The Ambassador closed his eyes and sighed. Nicholas Nelson should come in soon for his shift.

Axel wasn't expecting anything to happen to the Asters in the last ten minutes before the Emissary came to relieve him of his watch. But something did happen—and it wasn't anything good.

Axel's heart hammered in his chest as he stared at the television screen in the Board Room. One of the Asters' images was flickering dangerously quickly.

It wasn't the first time that Lian would suffer terrible injuries during a mission. As the Aster of Analgesia, he didn't realise half the time how bad his injuries were. On top of that, because of his courage and loyalty, Lian was often the one to take the brunt of an attack to protect his siblings.

During debriefing sessions after missions, Axel had heard this about Lian time and time again. And until now, the Aster had always found a way to survive. That didn't mean that the flickering image didn't send a spike of panic through Axel. Especially since there was nothing the Ambassador could do but watch the image and pray. He couldn't call upon the Ceders. He couldn't send Madeleine in with a vial of Sophie or

Katherine's blood. Because the Asters were in the Underworld, the Dark energy of the place was interfering with the Affinite technology that had gone into making the Asters' tracking chips. Axel didn't know if the vital signs that he was seeing reflected how Lian was right now, or if there was a delay in the signal. He also didn't know Lian's exact location, which meant he had no way of telling Madeleine where to shimmer to.

There was nothing he could do. It was up to the Asters themselves now. They were on their own.

For some reason Axel could see the location of Matu and Nathan. Those two were back out on the *Angel Trail*, while Sophie, Sky and Lian seemed to still be in the Underworld. Why the Asters had split up was a question Axel could only ask when all this was over. He would've loved to be able to call them, but at the pace they had been running only moments ago, it didn't seem like a good idea to distract them now.

Axel would have spent the next minutes with his eyes glued to the television screen if his phone hadn't started ringing. The Ambassador reached over and was about to decline the call, when he saw who was phoning him.

"David, what's the news?" Axel said by way of greeting. As the Affinite who had received the Asters and sent them down the Angel Trail, he might know more about the situation unfolding in the Grand Canyon.

"Your Asters managed to get seven of the fifteen missing hikers out. According to your oldest, Matu I believe, he and Nathan got them out while the other three created a diversion in the Underworld itself."

Well, that explained why the Asters had split up, Axel thought.

'The King was going to use the hikers for a re-opening of the fighting rings," David continued.

"The King? Mitrik is there?" Axel asked unbelievably.

"In person—I know. I didn't believe it either. He's got nerve, I'll say that much," David said.

Never in all the years that Axel had been Ambassador, had one of the seven Higher Kings shown his face on the Surface of the earth so brazenly. Axel wondered what game Mitrik was playing. He *had* been known to be cocky and rash, so Axel hoped that it wasn't a cover for tactical genius.

"What about the others? What do you know about Lian?" Axel asked.

"According to Matu, Lian showed up on the trail when Matu was about to be overwhelmed while holding back the Disciples so Nathan could work on their escape. Lian came just in time, and saved them, but got mortally wounded in the process. Matu and Nathan did have some vials of blood with them as they exited the Underworld, but lost them during combat with Disciples. Before Nathan and Matu got the hikers to me, Lian had already gone to find your girl to get healed. If Lian had waited a little while longer, he would've found out that I brought down one of their bags, which held the healer's blood," David explained. Axel swore to himself as David continued. "Your two boys are finding a way to get back down there to find Lian. My people are bringing the hikers back up to my office. I will take care of them and make sure they don't remember any of this—I should still have enough of the potions your scientists made. I will call you for more if not."

"Yes, that's fine," Axel said, trying to keep his voice under control. He couldn't keep his eyes off the television screen hanging above the corner desk. Lian's image was still flickering, but it was getting darker now. He was running out of time, and Axel had no way of knowing how near to Sophie he was. Lian had been so close to Sophie's blood... Of course, he had no way of knowing, but it still felt like a blow.

"I have a few of my crew who can join your boys, if you like. I will return and see if I can do something about disrupting that camp down below," David said.

The Disciple camp at the bottom of the Grand Canyon hadn't gone unnoticed. Mitrik had managed to get a small army together already. The Small Council had no way of knowing how many more Disciples there were just inside the Underworld, ready to spill out. It was impressive, what Mitrik had managed to do, though Axel still didn't understand the addition of the fighting rings. It didn't seem like something that would take priority in an attempt to reclaim the Surface. Capturing humans and re-opening the rings would only draw attention. Axel could only assume that Mitrik had done that on purpose. But to what end?

"Sir?" David sounded on the other end of the line.

The Ambassador shook himself, having been lost in thought. "Hm, yes, what?"

"Do you have any objections to me aiding your Asters?"

Axel shook his head, even though David couldn't see him. "Don't send anyone in with Nathan and Matu. Their priority is finding Lian, Sophie and Sky. Affinite help will most likely just slow them down. You can do what you can about the camp outside," Axel said. He'd have whoever Felix Hauser had as Mergers already in the North American Underworld to come and help the Asters, if they could without blowing their cover.

"Aye, Sir. I'll see what I can do," David said.

"Good. Thank you, David." Axel ended the call and looked at the screen again. Nothing had changed. Lian's image was still flickering terribly fast, but not faster than before. Axel wondered how long it would keep doing that before it would stop flickering and remain dark altogether. Experience told him not much longer...

Axel shook his head and turned his attention back to his phone. He had no control over what was happening to Lian in the North American Underworld right now. But he could possibly get him help. He dialled Felix's number. If there were any Mergers anywhere near the Grand Canyon, they might be in a position to help the Asters.

There was a knock on the door as Axel was about to make the call. He hesitated with his phone ready and called in whoever was on the other side of the door.

The door to the Board Room opened and Nicholas Nelson stepped inside. Axel had completely forgotten it was time for the Emissary to relieve Axel of his shift. The second Nicholas caught sight of the Ambassador, he could read everything on Axel's face.

"What's happened?" he asked.

Axel motioned to the television screen. "Lian's dying."

Nicholas studied the screen for a second. The image was getting dangerously dark now. Any minute now the image would be too dark to see and the flickering would stop. "How long has he been like that?" Nicholas asked.

"Longer than ever before," Axel muttered. He hit his fist hard on the desk. He hated sitting in this chair in these moments. He had no idea how far behind the signal was. He had no idea if Lian was okay already, or if he was already dead.

Axel turned his attention back to his phone again and called the Spymaster. It was the only thing he could do to help the Asters at this point. And he'd be damned if he didn't do everything he could to make sure that, of the five Asters he sent in, all five would also make it back out again.

Chapter 2

"Sky! Lian needs you!" Matu shouted.

Nothing happened. It was the third time Matu had called out his brother's name, but still Sky didn't come. The implications of that weren't good. Especially after Matu had tried to use Sky's blood to shimmer to Lian. Tried and failed.

"Sky!" he called once more, and waited.

No one came.

Matu sighed loudly and dropped to his knees beside Nathan. "He's not coming," he said.

"And that means?" Nathan asked absently. His brother was rummaging through the weapons bag that David Hughes' son, Jason, had brought with him down the *Angel Trail.* The Affinites had left with the human hikers a while ago.

"It means he can't hear me," Matu said. "Which means he can't hear Lian either."

"Which means Lian is probably still dying and can't get to Sophie in time," Nathan finished.

Matu glanced at his brother. The Band on his wrist was still glowing green, but Matu had no idea why Nathan was using his magic at this moment. He didn't want to ask. All he wanted was to find a way to get to Lian in time. They had Sophie's blood here, which meant they could use it and harness her magic long enough to heal Lian. Now all they needed was to actually *find* him.

"Do we even want to think about *why* Sky can't hear us?" Matu was trying to keep the anxiety out of his voice. He closed his eyes. He was the rational one of the Asters. The calm one. But he didn't feel calm now. Lian had never been so close to dying before. Not when he couldn't get to Sophie. Matu always knew there was a chance one of them could die on a mission. But not this one... Not Lian. Not while he was all alone in some tunnel in the Underworld. Not like this.

"The veil is gone," Nathan said matter-of-factly. "Our magic should surpass the Dark magic in the Underworld. Sky should be able to hear us. He and Sophie must be somewhere that is more heavily protected."

"*I know that.*"

"Then why did you ask?" Nathan asked absently. Matu had to bite back an angry remark at how emotionless Nathan was being even though Lian was incredibly close to dying right now. He knew this was how Nathan was on missions, but right now it was annoying.

Nathan pulled out a map from the bag and unfolded it onto his lap. The two of them looked at it. It was a map of the Grand Canyon's district of the Underworld.

"Plenty of detail, but it's still too big for us to pinpoint him," Nathan commented, casting the map aside. He took to rummaging through the large duffel bag again.

Matu threw up his hands in exasperation and stared at the blue sky. "We have Sky's blood. We can shimmer *anywhere* we want to. Why don't we just go down to where we last saw Sky and Sophie and try and track Lian again from there?"

"This Underworld is like any other. Our magic works as well up here to get in, as if we would use it down there. If we can't track him from here, we won't down there, either," Nathan said.

"Then what do we do? We don't have much time. He'll be dead soon. I told you of his injuries."

"Explicitly," Nathan replied.

Matu narrowed his eyes at his brother, but decided to say nothing.

"Here," Nathan said. He pulled out a few energy bars and a bottle of water from the bag and offered them all to Matu. It was only when Matu saw the water that he realised how thirsty he was. He took the bottle and drank deeply. Nathan pulled out a second bottle for himself.

Matu sat down next to Nathan. He moved slowly; his injured knee was still giving him trouble. It wasn't something he had time to focus on right now. He set down the water bottle and unwrapped the energy bar. "We have to find Lian before he bleeds to death, and that is before we start thinking about what is happening to Sky and Sophie."

"We don't have time to worry about Sky and Sophie," Nathan said simply. He grabbed a bag of trail mix and set it down in between himself and Matu.

Matu groaned in frustration. "No, I know that."

From his rummaging, Nathan pulled out the glass vials of Sky and Sophie's blood. It was as Matu said; they had the ability to travel anywhere in the world, and heal any injury.

"We need to break through whatever is blocking our connection to Lian," Matu murmured to himself. Then something occurred to him. "Nate."

Nathan looked up at his brother.

"Lian's blood is in there, too, right?" Matu asked.

After a few seconds of further rummaging through the bag, Nathan revealed a third vial of blood. "What are you thinking?" he asked.

"We have access to the magic of all five Asters. If we can combine all of them, it should be strong enough to break through whatever has been blocking us so far," Matu explained excitedly. "We cast a tracking spell with all five at the same time, and once the connection is stable, we use Sky's magic to shimmer right to him."

Nathan nodded slowly.

"It could work, right?" Matu said.

Nathan thought for a moment. "It could."

"All right!" Matu said eagerly. He jumped up, completely forgetting about his injured knee. Pain shot through his leg and he stumbled. Matu caught a hold of the rock wall to steady himself.

"We need to heal that first," Nathan said. His Band was still glowing. What bit of nature was he connected to, Matu wondered. What was he using his magic for? But Matu didn't want to ask.

"Fine, but hurry," Matu said, stepping gingerly towards Nathan.

As Nathan unplugged the vial of Sophie's blood, Matu glanced down the trail. Only a few feet away from them the path had crumbled apart completely. The trail resumed far below them. At least fifteen Disciples were still down there, staring up at them, letting the Asters know that they couldn't go back down that way without expecting a fight. It was only thanks to Lian's efforts of holding them off that Nathan and Matu had managed to escape and get the humans out safely. If it hadn't been for Lian, they'd all have been killed.

"*Excipie magica sanitatis*," Nathan was saying.

Matu tore his eyes away from the Disciples and looked at how a second Band appeared next to Nathan's already glowing one. The replica of Sophie's Band started glowing golden, and Nathan placed his hand on Matu's knee. Matu could feel the warmth of Sophie's magic through his whole body. It didn't just heal his injured knee, but also the wound on his collar bone where the Disciple had cut through the strap of the backpack.

When Nathan was finished, he pulled his hand away, and Sophie's Band disappeared. His own Band still glowed. Matu looked down at his brother and, for the first time, noticed the exhaustion on Nathan's face. Matu hadn't forgotten the immensity of the magic Nathan had performed to get them there. Making the tunnels through the Underworld and the staircase out of thin air must have taken such energy.

Matu crouched down beside his brother. "Hey, Nate," he said.

Nathan looked up at him. The coldness still hadn't left him, but his tiredness was clear.

"Just a little longer, all right? We can rest once we save Lian," Matu said. "Can you hang on long enough for that?"

Nathan looked at him with those focused eyes. "Of course," he said.

"All right, then. Give me the vials," he said.

Nathan leaned over the bag and took the three vials of Sophie, Sky and Lian's blood. He turned to Matu, but hesitated in giving them to him. He glanced at his own Band, still glowing.

"What's wrong? We don't have much time," Matu said, holding out his hands.

But Nathan pulled his hands back. "If you do this then you'll break the magic protecting Lian," he said.

"Protecting? No, blocking. Something is blocking Lian," Matu said. "Give me the vials, Nate."

Nathan shook his head, and looked up at Matu. "You can't cast this spell. Lian will die if you do."

"What are you talking about?"

Nathan turned away from Matu and put down the vials of Sophie and Lian's blood.

"Nate!" Matu exclaimed. "What are you doing?" He leaned over to try and grab the vials of blood, but Nathan, with more strength than Matu expected, pushed him back.

"You have to trust me," Nathan said. He held the vial of Sky's blood in his hands.

"What?"

"You couldn't shimmer to Lian because something was blocking you, right?"

"Well, yes."

"I think I know what was blocking you. And I think I know how to get past it."

Nathan started unscrewing the vial and was about to bring it to his lips, when Matu stopped him.

"You are near exhaustion. You don't have the energy to do another spell like this. Tell me what to do, and I'll do it," Matu said. He forced himself to remain calm. He trusted his brother, even though he had no idea what was going on in Nathan's head right now. This might be the absolute worst time to trust him, but Matu couldn't help being convinced by that focus in Nathan's eyes. Nathan suspected something.

Nathan shook his head. "You have to trust me. You can't get to him; I can."

"Nate..."

"We don't have any other choice!"

Matu closed his eyes and thought for as long as he dared to. Lian was dying and needed them now. Nathan was close to exhaustion, and another big spell could kill him. But if they didn't get to Lian in the next few minutes, his injuries would kill him. Matu had to take the risk. He had to let Nathan execute his plan.

Matu made his decision. He stared straight at Nathan. "I trust you," he said.

Nathan didn't waste another second. He grabbed the vial with Sophie's blood and gave it to Matu, who placed it in the inside pocket of his jacket. Matu reached into the bag, grabbed another few energy bars and shoved them in another pocket. He also grabbed a full water bottle. Even if they managed to save Lian from his injuries, his body still needed food and drink to regain its full strength.

Nathan brought the vial of Sky's blood to his lips and took a small sip. Matu looked at his brother. Nathan had his eyes closed.

One second passed.

Then another.

16

Nathan swallowed, and whispered, "*Excipie magica celeritatis.*"
A Band just like Sky's appeared on his wrist. Matu stared at the Band.
It was still black. Nathan wasn't harnessing Sky's magic yet.
Matu looked up and found that his brother was frowning.
And then part of Sky's Band started changing colour.
It wasn't an outright shine, but the black lines were turning lighter.
Matu forced himself to remain calm. The fact that Nathan couldn't
harness Sky's magic outright, proved once again how tired he already
was. But it was working. He was concentrating with every fibre of his
body, and it was working.

Lian's wounds were still so clear in Matu's mind. Every time he
blinked, he could see Lian on the back of his eyelids, one hand on his
stomach, while using the single dagger in his other hand to fight. Only
Lian could still move with injuries like that. Only Lian would survive so
long with injuries like that. And he was still alive; he had to be.

Matu held on to that thought as he stared at the two Bands on Nathan's
wrist. The Band that belonged to Sky's magic was slowly changing
colour. It was getting brighter. It was just a small glimmer first, but it
was getting stronger, and it was starting to shine. And soon enough,
the Band that symbolised Sky's magic was glowing just as brightly as
Matu knew it should.

Nathan held out his hand for Matu to take. Matu did so, and was about
to whisper to his brother that he was doing great, but his words were
stolen from him. From one moment to the next he was swept away. A
brilliant blue light appeared all around them and the ground underneath
him disappeared.

Matu gripped Nathan's hand tighter as the two of them flew through
space. The shimmer took longer than when Sky did it. But they were
shimmering nonetheless.

The bright light started to soften, and Matu once again felt the ground
underneath him. When the light of the shimmer vanished completely,

Matu blinked a few times. He realised that he was still in a crouching position. He looked around. The bright sunlight was replaced with the dim flicker of lanterns attached to the tunnel walls of the Underworld. He dropped the water bottle he was holding.

"We're in!" Matu exclaimed. He didn't realise that the hand he was still holding didn't have any strength in it. He was too busy looking for Lian. Matu spun his head around and looked every which way. They were in a corridor—a side corridor. A few feet away from him to his right was a door, and to his left an intersection with a larger hallway.

But there was no Lian.

Matu let go of Nathan's hand, jumped to his feet and sped to the door first, and pulled on it. The door wouldn't budge. While cursing his stupidity, Matu focused for a moment and used his magic of Strength to yank the door open. It led to a small room with a large rectangular table in the middle and a few chairs around it. Matu knelt down to see if Lian was lying anywhere on the floor.

He wasn't.

"Matu..."

Matu spun around and stared at Nathan. His brother still knelt in the exact spot as where he had appeared after the shimmer. He was bent slightly forward, and it looked like he was about to be ill.

"I can't see him. Where is he? Didn't it work?" Matu stammered. He stared past Nathan but they were alone in the corridor. Lian was nowhere to be seen.

Nathan tried to get up, but Matu could see that there was no energy left in Nathan's body. He would have fallen forward to the ground if Matu hadn't come over to steady him.

"Woah, stay with me," Matu urged as he caught his brother before he fell.

Nathan leaned heavily against Matu. Sky's Band had vanished from his wrist. His own Band was still pulsing green, but much less brightly than it had before.

"Lian..." Nathan whispered. His eyes fluttered. And the strength left his body completely. If Matu hadn't had his arm around him, Nathan would've tumbled to the ground. He hadn't lost consciousness completely, but his tanned skin had grown pale and his eyelids were drooping. Matu cursed; he should never have had him cast that last spell. Now two of his brothers were at death's door, exactly what he'd feared would happen.

"Lian..." Nathan whispered again.

Matu looked around frantically. Lian was nowhere to be seen, and he couldn't leave his brother like this to go and investigate further. Matu looked down at Nathan. He was trying to push himself up, but he couldn't manage it.

Matu held on to Nathan with one hand and fumbled in his jacket to find the vial that contained Sophie's blood. At least he would be able to heal any physical injuries Nathan had sustained; it would buy time for his body to resist the potentially fatal fatigue from Nathan's over-use of magic.

Lian was nowhere near them. Matu forced himself to focus on the task at hand, which was saving Nathan. He tried not to think about what it meant that the spell hadn't worked and that Lian was bleeding out, possibly somewhere very close to them.

Either way their brother was going to die, and he was going to be completely alone when he did.

Chapter 3

Sky and Sophie followed Mitrik down the path to the white castle. Their hands were still bound in the North American King's magical white bonds, but apart from that they were free to move. It was the knowledge that Mitrik could increase the tightness of the bonds, or could wrap the bonds around them completely with the wave of a hand, that stopped either one of them from trying to break free. Their weapons had also been taken from them and tossed over the edge of the marble path into the chasm beneath.

All Sophie could think about was Lian. Ever since Sky had told her that Lian had called for him, Sophie had a horrible feeling in the pit of her stomach. It took all her effort not to show her fear and stress. It wasn't fear for her own life; if Mitrik hadn't killed her and Sky the second he found them, then he wasn't going to kill them any time soon. Which meant they had time. Time to plan and calculate an escape. But how much time did Lian have? How close was he to Matu and Nathan? Matu had her blood in the backpack.

With all of her being, Sophie hoped that the second Sky didn't answer his call, Lian would go back and find Matu. That would be the best decision. If Sky didn't answer a call, that meant that Sky was in trouble. And if Lian needed Sophie, that meant he was in no state to fight off whatever trouble Sky and Sophie might be in. Even with his magic, Lian couldn't risk having to fight. Not if he was specifically calling Sky for

Sophie.

Sophie kept her eyes on the man in front of her. She put all her effort into trusting that Lian, Matu and Nathan would be all right without her; for as long as it would take for her and Sky to come up with an escape plan. Well, for her alone to come up with an escape plan, she corrected herself with grim humour, planning and strategy not being Sky's strong points.

Sophie glanced briefly beside her to her brother. He had his eyes on the King as well. Mitrik's liquid silver hair was unlike anything she had ever seen before. Sophie knew that every King had something unnatural about them; something that made them no longer entirely human. For Mitrik it had been the touch of silver, just like every one of his predecessors. His hair shimmered eerily in the light of the lanterns. If the King turned around, Sophie knew his silver eyes would glint unnaturally in the same way.

Sophie tried to move her hands against the bonds around her wrists, but they wouldn't budge. The bonds were uncomfortable and painfully tight. She knew that she wouldn't be able to break them. Mitrik was the only one who could take them off her, and it was obvious he wasn't going to anytime soon. The only way for her and Sky to get free, was if Mitrik voluntarily removed the bonds himself. Or if he died, which meant his magic would dissipate. Sophie knew for a fact that Sky was pondering how to achieve the latter possibility. Every time she looked at her brother, she could see the violence he was planning in his eyes.

For a moment Sky looked back at her. Sophie frowned at him and shook her head, trying to make clear to him, without using words, that violence was not the fastest way out of here. Sky stared angrily back at her, mouthing Lian's name to her. Sophie shook her head even more vigorously. She wanted to get out of here as much as he did. They both knew the worst possible outcome if Lian was alone somewhere and couldn't get to them, or to Nathan and Matu.

Sophie knew that Mitrik wasn't a fighter—he never had been. But that didn't mean that he could be killed easily. Especially while they were still in these bonds. And definitely not with the two Disciples walking behind Sophie and Sky, hands on their weapons if either one of the Asters dared set a foot out of place.

One of the Disciples was male and the other female. They were both dressed in black armour that was lined with white. Their weapons were white, too. The Disciples outside on the Canyon floor hadn't had white weapons. Theirs had been regular black and iron, with a little bit of white mixed in with the black of the hilts. But the weapons these two Disciples were carrying... both hilt and blade alike were ghostly white. That was an indication of a higher ranking if ever Sophie saw one.

There had been something about the female Disciple, in particular, that unnerved Sophie. She radiated something that Sophie couldn't quite place. She was in her late twenties, if Sophie had to guess. She had blonde hair, but it was already streaked heavily with grey, even at such a young age. It was tied in a single thick braid down her back. She had thick, black make-up around her eyes, which made her pale grey eyes stand out. But it wasn't her appearance that agitated Sophie. It was something different. Something *more* than any other Disciple Sophie had ever encountered before. It was like her aura was tangible.

Sophie glanced over her shoulder and looked at the female Disciple. She stared back, her face stone cold. Sophie turned her head back. They had reached the drawbridge at the end of the marble path. Looking up, Sophie saw that the castle itself stood on far higher ground. Below and around it, the castle was surrounded by a small township made up of shimmering white buildings. All around the lowest level, where they were standing now, a great high wall encircled the stronghold, with this single drawbridge leading away from it. Walking along the marble path, Sophie remembered seeing a similar path leading away from the other side. Up ahead, beyond the drawbridge, was a cobblestone path, leading into the town and, presumably, towards the entrance of the castle.

"Welcome to my home," Mitrik said, raising his arms in front of him and gesturing at the immense architectural structure in front of him. He turned around and looked at Sophie and Sky, his silver eyes shining. "I don't believe you've ever been here before? Would you like a tour?"

Sophie stared at the King disbelievingly.

He looked to be in his early thirties, but Sophie knew that the King was at least seventy years old. Aside from the South American King, Mitrik was the youngest of the Seven Higher Kings.

"I'd rather know why you haven't killed us yet," Sky said. Sophie could kick him... She guessed she should be glad he'd accepted to *not* try and kill Mitrik the first chance they got, but she wasn't sure mimicking Mitrik's arrogant nonchalance was the best way to keep a possibly bloodthirsty King calm.

Mitrik cocked his head to the left and pursed his lips. "Would you like to be killed?" he asked.

"I would prefer to stay alive," Sky replied. She forced her face to remain neutral. Leave it to Sky to go from one extreme to the other. Of course it wasn't possible for him to find an attitude somewhere in the middle...

"Well, then," Mitrik mused. "What is the problem? You Asters are never grateful for anything are you? You don't want to die, and I'm not killing you. Why question it?"

Mitrik turned on his heels and pointed up ahead. "This way," he said chirpily.

Sophie and Sky followed Mitrik across the drawbridge. Sky leaned in towards Sophie and whispered, "I question it because he's the one making all the decisions."

"Shut up," Sophie hissed back.

"I heard that," Mitrik called over his shoulder. "You know that we Kings think that you Asters make all the decisions. Funny how that works, right? One man's terrorist is another man's freedom fighter, and all that. We can think the same things and both be right. Or both be wrong, I suppose. Whichever way you want to look at it. I like to see it as both being right. Makes my outlook a lot more positive than my six brothers. My, my, what a brooding bunch are they. Though they are not my brothers by blood, of course. But you two know all about that, don't you?"

As it was rhetorical, neither of them answered the King's question. It was obvious he was prattling more to himself than to anyone else around him. Of all that Sophie had heard about the North American King, she certainly hadn't expected this. While he was known not to be a fighter, Sophie had expected to come face to face with a tactical mastermind, planning and plotting his every move. Manipulating them along the way, and very subtly fitting pieces together. Something similar to what the unknown South American King had done. *Those* were actions that Sophie would've associated with Mitrik. She hadn't expected this chatty, laid back and grinning man, who distinctly reminded her of David Hughes.

As they followed the North American King down the white cobblestone path, Sophie looked up at the glittering buildings around her. The phrase *looks can be deceiving* had never applied to anything as much as it did here. The white bricks that made up every wall and street within Mitrik's castle looked pure and welcoming. If there weren't Disciples walking around, Sophie could almost mistake these streets for the white rock streets of Santorini in Greece.

Up ahead, the path turned into stairs. Mitrik continued to prattle as he led them up higher. At a platform Mitrik left the staircase and stepped onto the battlements. The King beckoned them to the low stone wall. Sky and Sophie took their place next to the King and looked outward. The female Disciple made a point of standing right behind Sky. Sophie saw Sky noting the Disciple's presence behind him, and

Sophie realised that killing Mitrik quickly was still in the back of Sky's mind, if the opportunity presented itself. With the element of surprise, Sky might have succeeded in throwing the King over the edge of the battlements. Sadly, he wouldn't get the chance now that the female Disciple anticipated the possible attempt. Thankfully, even Sky wasn't stupid enough to try anyway.

Down below, Sophie could see the marble path that wound all the way to the large white and iron door in the Canyon wall that Sky had supported her through earlier. Only from up here could she see that the path was built upon a large assembly of stalagmites. On either side of the path was an immense drop, so dark that Sophie couldn't begin to calculate how far down the fall would be. Instead of dwelling on that thought, she looked up and saw what looked like icicles made of rock, covering the entirety of the cavern ceiling. The mass of stalactites looked both beautiful and daunting. There was something breath-takingly dramatic about the natural rock formation around them.

"Nice view, isn't it?" Mitrik asked. "My ancestors weren't too shabby when it came to architecture. Not like some of my brothers, *ugh*, they live in an absolute cave."

The King laughed. He looked over at Sophie and Sky and his laugh faded away. "You do understand the joke, right? You're supposed to laugh at jokes."

Sophie and Sky stared long and hard at the King. Was he serious?

"I've heard better jokes," Sky replied.

The King grinned and pointed at Sophie's brother. "I'm sure you have. I'm sure you've seen better views than this, too, right? I've only heard stories of that castle of yours."

Mitrik made a large gesture with his arms. "Built into the cliffs, with names chiselled into the rock of every fallen Affinite from the Original War, and a view over the entire island and the sea. Or was it an ocean? Remind me, where was that island of yours again?"

Sophie kept her face a mask of neutrality, though she had trouble concealing her continued surprise at the personality this King was showing. She had expected someone dark and sinister with no conscience. And yet the way Mitrik talked, there was something almost human about him. The thought of it sent a chill down her spine.

Sky said nothing either. For as long as Saluverus had existed, it had been kept secret from Disciples and Kings; its precise location in the Norwegian Sea made undetectable by its magically protective Curtain.

Mitrik grinned again, his teeth as white as pearls. "You two were trained well. It was worth a shot, right? Can never dream too big, I always say." He leaned in closer and said in a low voice, "You know, I dream of getting out of here and seeing the ocean. With that cool air all around me; I'd feel so free. That's what I want more than anything. I'm sure that's what anybody wants."

Sophie stared at the King, utterly shocked at the simplicity of his dream. And the fact that he was telling them this. Asters and Affinites were brought up believing the Kings were truly evil, with no emotions or conscience, and only caring about one thing: world domination and oppression. But here Mitrik stood, just wanting that simple thing he couldn't have because of what he was born to be. Ironic, that domination would probably be the only way he'd have the freedom to live that dream.

It seemed obvious at first that Mitrik would only lie about this to get Sophie and Sky to have sympathy for him. And maybe that was his plan. But there was something in his eyes when he spoke of the ocean that told her it wasn't all artifice. Perhaps far below the surface, under all the liquid silver hair, the ageless eyes and the powerful magic, was still a boy with a dream. Of a way he wanted his life to be if he had a choice.

As quickly as Mitrik had used a deeper, more emotional voice, he switched back to his light and chirpy ways. He practically jumped back up and said, "And I need you two to get it! Right, anyway, let's keep going."

Mitrik stepped away from the castle battlements and headed back towards the cobblestone staircase. Sophie and Sky followed, all the while being closely watched by the two Disciples behind them.

The staircase led up to the gates of the castle high above. Mitrik raised his hands above his head and said, "Welcome to my home. I would give you a tour, but you don't seem to be in such a good mood, and I prefer more *chatty* company. You two are too serious, you know that, right? We could have a cup of tea in my private quarters, the three of us. We could talk about our work, share life stories, plans for the future, all that kind of thing."

Mitrik looked over his shoulder and studied both of them. "No?"

They both kept their faces neutral and said nothing. Two guards opened each side of the gate and they all waited for Mitrik to keep going. But he remained where he was for a moment.

"Well, then. I have tried to be friendly, you know? Trying to be a good host and all that. But if you're so keen to be treated like dirt, well..." Mitrik's silver eyes suddenly turned sly and they slid from Sky to Sophie. They trailed up and down Sophie's body and rested on her face. "I could also treat you the way my Disciples treat all other pretty girls like you."

Sophie's face warmed.

Sky advanced immediately. "You son of a—"

A second later he had a knife at his throat.

The female Disciple had shot forward, faster than Sophie had ever seen a Disciple move. She pressed the knife hard against Sky's throat and a few drops of blood stained the bone white blade.

Mitrik chuckled. Sky was seething with anger. Sophie had her jaw clenched as she forced herself to keep her mouth shut. Mitrik wanted to see the fear in her; the power he had over her. With these magical bonds, Mitrik could keep her from moving, and do whatever he liked with her. But she wouldn't show him how afraid she was. She wouldn't give the King that satisfaction. Even though she was downright terrified, she made sure she didn't show her panic. She was smarter than that. Unlike Sky, she was smart enough not to charge at the King.

"Oh, you are nothing if not utterly predictable." Mitrik clicked his tongue, and then turned to look at Sky. "You should've been smarter than coming at me, boy. If my beautiful Third hadn't cut your throat, I certainly would've had my fun. Please, Kali, dear, release the *adorably* protective boy."

Sophie watched as the female Disciple slowly removed the white knife from Sky's throat and stepped back.

"You see, Kali is just as protective of me. Just like you are protective of her," Mitrik told Sky, nodding towards Sophie. "You and I are not as different as you would make us out to be, you know. Like I said, perspective is everything. Funny thing that is, funny thing. I do like irony. There is so much irony in the world, don't you think? It does keep life a little more interesting." He twirled around and stepped through the gates. After a pause, during which Sophie glared at her brother for being so unnecessarily and uselessly protective, she and Sky followed the King through.

A tall, white door with iron hinges rose up in front of them. It swung open without a sound as they approached. They stepped into a grand entrance hall, with marble pillars along the walls. Beige and silver rugs covered the floor, and paintings of various coastal views and seascapes hung on the walls. A large, glass, helical staircase stood in the middle. Mitrik turned a sharp right. He pressed a button on the wall next to the entrance doors and a trapdoor swung open at his feet, revealing another set of stairs. Mitrik turned around and looked past Sophie and Sky.

"Kali, my dear. Would you escort my guests to their rooms?" the King said.

"Of course, my King," Kali said behind them.

Mitrik clapped his hands. "Excellent. There is so much to do. So many plans to make. Oh, the plans I have for you! I was so lucky that you stumbled into my cavern—saved me the effort of having to go after you myself. Ah, the time you saved me, thank you my friends."

Mitrik stepped away from the trapdoor and headed towards the helical staircase. When he reached the bottom step, he turned around. "Oh, there was one more thing."

He raised his right hand in front of him and formed it into a fist. It started glowing white, and suddenly Sky's breathing hitched. Sophie looked at her brother, and saw that a white band, just like the ones around their wrists, had appeared around Sky's throat. And it was tightening slowly.

His breathing became even more strained, until almost no air was getting in at all. Sky brought his bonded hands up and clawed at his throat. The choking sounds that came from him was too much for Sophie to bear. She tried to get to Sky, but the male Disciple advanced and put a knife to her throat. The blade pressed hard against her skin, and she knew he would have no trouble killing her if she made another move towards her brother.

"Stop it!" Sophie yelled. She reached for Sky anyway, but Kali quickly stepped in between Sophie and Sky as well. Now both Disciples separated the two of them. Sophie couldn't go anywhere near her brother as he fell to his knees, his hands clawing at his throat. He then dropped onto his side. His lips started turning blue and his eyes, which had been darting around frantically, started to bulge and roll upwards.

"Sky!" Sophie screamed.

The energy seemed to vanish from his body; the movement of his hands at the band around his neck slowed, and then stilled. His entire body stilled completely.

"NO!" Sophie could only watch as the life drained out of her brother. Not like this... not this way. Not when Lian still needed their help. There had to be something she could do. Sophie searched Kali's face, but the eyes of Mitrik's third-in-command were stone cold as she watched Sky die at her feet.

Sophie was about to brave the drawn weapons of Mitrik's Second and Third, when suddenly the band around Sky's throat vanished, and he heaved in a huge breath. He coughed and spluttered, but he was alive. Sky put his bonded hands beneath him and raised himself up slightly. He looked over at Mitrik, a fire burning in his eyes. Sophie did the same. The King was still standing at the bottom of the helical stairway. The white light around his fist had vanished and he slowly lowered his hand. His silver eyes had lost all their humour and were now icy cold, as he stared at Sky.

"Just because I am not a fighter, does not mean I rely on my Second and Third to do all my dirty work. I can very well protect myself. It will do you good to remember that. In your bonds you do not stand a chance against me," Mitrik said. He talked slowly, enunciating every single word with deafening clarity.

The King of the North American Underworld then turned his head to look at his Third. "Take them away."

Chapter 4

Matu finally freed the vial of Sophie's blood from his inside jacket pocket. Even in his exhausted state, Nathan was still struggling to push himself up onto his knees.

"Keep still," Matu commanded. He didn't want to lose one brother today. Let alone two. But Nathan wouldn't keep still. It even seemed as though some strength had returned to his muscles, because Nathan managed to roll off of Matu's legs and to the side.

"Nate!" Matu hissed. But Nathan didn't have eyes for him. He pushed himself up so that he was resting on his hands and knees. His arms were shaking, but they were stronger than before. Nathan lifted his left hand, so that he was only balancing on his right, and pointed past Matu. The Band on Nathan's wrist, that had still been glowing dimly in the lantern light, suddenly flared up again. Matu turned away from Nathan to follow the direction of his finger. At first, he seemed to be pointing at nothing. The line from his finger led to a patch of uneven rock at the bottom of the wall, no more than fifty feet away from them. It bulged out onto the floor slightly. It was nothing more than a shallow bump. The same as every wall of every tunnel in this Underworld.

But then the bump started rippling, and Matu realised that he wasn't looking at a slab of uneven rock, but at vines of the same dark brown colour.

"No..." Matu breathed in disbelief. On his hands and knees, Matu crawled towards the brown vines as they continued to ripple and morph. At first, they seemed to be growing out of the wall, but then Matu saw that they weren't growing, but moving away from it. The vines continued to move like a nest of snakes; each and every one of them alive and shifting, until an entire cocoon of brown vines was lying free, right in front of Matu's knees. The cocoon was as long as a man, and as the vines started to uncurl, Matu could see parts of a person completely encased within. He could just make out the black Aster gear through the untangling vines.

Matu caught his breath as he recognised the short, spiky hair, and the tone of Lian's skin.

Matu looked back at Nathan incredulously. His brother was still on his hands and knees. His arms were still shaking and he was panting hard, but his Band was glowing true. Nathan nodded and Matu felt an almighty surge of emotion.

Could it be true? Could Lian still be alive?

Matu turned back to the cocoon in front of him. The tightness of the vines must have helped staunch the bleeding. Maybe enough to keep Lian alive.

Matu moved to the middle of the long cocoon, the vial of Sophie's blood at the ready. He took a sip of the blood and said quickly, "*Excipie magica sanitates.*"

A Band identical to Sophie's appeared on Matu's wrist. Matu held that same hand over the slowly unravelling cocoon of vines. Even in this nearly depleted state, Nathan was controlling the unfurling with exquisite timing, waiting for Matu to be ready to heal. They both knew Lian could possibly only have seconds between the vines being gone and him bleeding to death.

Usually when Matu harnessed Sophie's magic he closed his eyes. He kept them open this time. He needed to place his hand on the worst injury; that was where the magic needed to flow through strongest first.

He held his hand steady and focused on the foreign magic in his body. He could feel the warmth of Sophie's magic coursing through his veins. He could feel it move from his entire body, through just his right arm, and down into his hand and right into his fingertips.

"Ready," he told Nathan.

The vines split open in the middle, revealing Lian's torn and bleeding abdomen. Immediately, blood gushed out of the wound. Matu wasted no time. He placed his hand just on the edge of the wound and allowed Sophie's magic to shoot from his fingers and do its work on Lian. Matu didn't even know if Lian was still breathing. His chest wasn't visibly moving up and down anymore. But the magic still shot from his hand into Lian's body. Matu could see the intestines move back into place. He never enjoyed this part of the job. How Sophie could look at hundreds of injuries like these without passing out or throwing up, Matu would never know.

But Matu kept his eyes firmly on Lian's abdomen. The vines continued to loosen around Lian's body, but Matu forced himself not to look up at Lian's face. He would only look when he knew most of the healing had been done. So far, the healing was going well. The abdominal wall was knitting itself back together, and the edges of the torn skin on either side of the wound were growing steadily towards each other.

Behind him, Matu heard Nathan pull himself closer. Matu knew he would have to move on to Nathan the second he was finished with Lian. In the past hour, Nathan had exhibited such immense strength; more than Matu had ever seen from his brother. He had no idea Nathan's power could go to these lengths, and Matu wondered if Nathan had even known himself. It was certainly taking its toll right now.

The healing magic continued to flow out of Matu's hand in strong waves. The outer layer of skin was almost closed up now, and Matu dared to look at Lian's face. The brilliance of Sophie's magic was that she never had to heal every single injury. The magic would run from her hand into the body of the recipient, and wherever there were injuries, no matter the size, the magic would heal it all in one swoop.

There was only dried blood left on Lian's face. There were no cuts or gashes to be seen. His eyes were firmly closed and so was his mouth. Matu still couldn't tell if his brother was breathing, but he found comfort in remembering that Sophie had told him that she couldn't heal the dead. Her magic wouldn't even leave her hands then. That knowledge gave Matu all the hope he needed.

Underneath his fingers, the wound to Lian's abdomen had healed completely. Matu moved his non-healing hand to Lian's chest. Very softly, Matu could feel the thumps of Lian's heart. They weren't strong beats, but that didn't matter. Sophie's magic was doing its job, and as it was still working its way through Lian's body, there was nothing more Matu could do for his brother, other than wait for that heart to beat stronger on its own.

The second Matu was sure of this, he turned to Nathan. He was now lying on the ground beside Matu. He didn't even have the strength anymore to kneel. His eyes were closed and his breaths were shallow. As Sophie's magic coursed through Matu again, he could feel the utter exhaustion within his brother. Sophie's magic was for healing physical injuries, not fatigue. Nathan barely had any wounds because he had been creating the escape; not fighting the Disciples. But he must have sustained some damage to his muscles and bone from the effort of fashioning the tunnel and staircase, because Nathan seemed to be responding to Sophie's magic. His exhaustion seemed to be easing, if only just a little.

"How did you do that?" Matu asked, referring to the vine cocoon.

Nathan's eyes fluttered open and he held Matu's gaze for a moment. "I didn't... know I could," he panted.

"Then how?"

Nathan closed his eyes for a moment. "I sent my magic... into the

CHAPTER 4

earth... It's almost impossible... every inch... of this place... is infected with Dark...magic." Nathan paused for a moment to take a shaky breath. "But I made my magic... search for... my brother... and keep him alive..."

Matu took away his hand. He'd hoped that Sophie's magic would return some of the colour to Nathan's face, but it hadn't. He still looked exhausted, but not as much as before.

"That's why I couldn't track Lian and you could," Matu realised. "Your magic was protecting him—blocking everything. Only your magic could reach him through its own cocoon."

Nathan slowly opened his eyes again. They weren't as cold as Matu was used to when they were on missions; a light was dancing in them, ever so slightly.

"I can't believe that worked," Matu breathed.

Nathan smiled at him weakly. Matu hugged him tightly. He was in awe of his youngest brother's brilliance and power. For a moment, Matu couldn't help but tip his head to the ceiling and smile.

A groan.

Matu turned his head. Nathan looked as well. Lian was opening his eyes slowly. He looked around, trying to get his bearings. He found Matu and met his gaze. Lian moved an arm and placed his hand on his stomach. Something flickered in his eyes as he felt the clean, new skin where a gaping wound had been. Lian placed his arms on either side of him and pushed himself up to a sitting position. He looked around, realising only Matu and Nathan were in the corridor.

Lian rubbed his eyes with one hand and let out a long breath. When he opened them again and he looked from one brother to the other, he asked, "Anybody going to tell me how the hell I'm still alive?"

35

Nathan had lost consciousness seconds after Lian had awoken. Matu wasn't that worried; Nathan's body just needed loads of rest to regain its strength. The only problem was that they were in the middle of the Underworld, in an unknown corridor, and with Sophie and Sky still possibly trapped someplace else.

"What happened to him?" Lian asked in between gulps of water from the bottle Matu had brought.

"Long story," Matu replied. Nathan was slumped against him.

"Will he be all right?"

"Should be. But I don't know when."

Matu looked from Nathan to Lian. Against all odds both brothers were safe and still alive. They didn't have time to talk about what a miracle that was. They had other things to worry about now.

"First, we need to get out of sight in case Disciples show up. There's a room over there." Matu gestured to the door at the end of the corridor. He used his magic to pick Nathan up without much effort. The Band on his wrist glowed bronze as he headed down the corridor. Lian was already there, holding the door open.

Lian closed the door behind them. Matu walked over to the rectangular table in the middle of the room and laid Nathan down on top of it.

"What are the odds that no one will find us before he wakes up?" Lian asked.

Matu looked around the room. There was a fine layer of dust on the table, chairs and the floor. It didn't seem like the room had been in use for a while.

"We need to lock that door," Matu said.

Lian nodded and turned to the handle. Matu pulled a chair away from the table and sat down on it. He looked at Nathan's face. His breathing had turned deep—a good sign. He was sleeping deeply while his body recovered. Behind him, Matu could hear Lian reciting the spell to lock doors. With it finished, only Lian would be able to open the door. They could only hope that Disciples, on finding this room locked, would just turn around and find another, instead of trying to break it down.

Lian walked over to the table and sat down on a chair next to Matu.

"It might be a while before he wakes up," Matu said. Nathan's face looked calm and peaceful.

"Matu," Lian said. Matu turned to his other brother and waited for the question. "How am I still alive?"

Before telling the story, Matu reached into his pocket and drew out the energy bars. He offered them to Lian. As his brother ate, Matu cleared his throat and told the whole story; from the moment Lian shimmered away from them after buying Matu time to climb onto Nathan's vine staircase, to the moment Nathan shimmered them to the corridor and revealing he'd somehow kept Lian alive from a distance by wrapping him in the cocoon of vines.

Lian looked absolutely gobsmacked when Matu had finished. "I didn't know he had that much power."

Matu managed to grin. "Neither did I."

Lian let out a low whistle.

They remained silent for a while. It didn't surprise Matu that Lian acted so normal after being so close to dying. He'd been close to death before; he was the only one of them who never seemed to fear it. Matu knew Lian would've welcomed death, knowing that his efforts had saved Matu and Nathan and the hikers. It was something Matu very much envied. He knew that any of them could die at any moment. Hell, they were somewhere in the North American Underworld right now. That fear of dying constantly bubbled somewhere low in Matu's gut, as he knew it did with them all.

"How close do you think he was to over-using his magic?" Lian asked, breaking the silence.

Matu looked up at Nathan's face. "No idea," he answered honestly. Nathan had been in such control during their escape outside. It was only when he wanted to be the one to shimmer to Lian, that Matu saw exhaustion was gripping him.

It wasn't like when Sophie had almost died over-using her magic earlier that year. She'd pushed on even when her body told her to stop. In contrast, Nathan had accepted his body forcing him to rest. If he'd pushed through that, as well, he might indeed have come close to dying.

"It was good that he didn't fight it," Matu said.

Lian nodded, knowing exactly what his brother was talking about. "Any idea how long he'll be out?"

Matu shook his head.

"So, we're stuck here until he wakes," Lian said.

Matu sighed. He was feeling suddenly very tired himself.

"We need to know when Disciples are coming before they start banging on this door," Matu said. He forced himself to his feet and walked to the door.

"And how do you propose we do that?" Lian asked.

Matu placed his hand on the door. "Do you remember one of our spell classes where Mrs Saito taught us something about a one-way door?"

"You know who you're talking to, right?" Lian leaned back in his chair. "Do you really expect me to remember that?"

Matu chuckled. "No, I don't. What was I thinking?"

"Do you remember?" Lian pointed out.

"It wasn't in the spell-reminder classes Sophie and Sylvia forced us to take," Matu mused. "I don't think I remember all the words."

Lian let out a sigh. "Then why did you bring it up? Since neither one of us know the spell?"

Matu smiled at Lian. "Because I know someone who does." He pulled the vial of Sophie's blood out of his pocket and dangled it in front of Lian so he could see.

"No way."

Matu shrugged. "If anyone knows..."

"We've only ever used that for healing. I wouldn't even know how to look for knowledge," Lian said.

"There's only one way to try," Matu replied. He opened the vial. It was still half full. Matu took a small sip and spoke the words of the incantation to harness Sophie's magic of Knowledge and Health. A Band identical to Sophie's appeared on his wrist.

"She's going to scorn me for forgetting," Matu muttered as he focused on Sophie's magic.

"Yeah, well, then she'd scorn all of us for forgetting so many things," Lian said.

Matu grinned as he closed his eyes. The second Band on his wrist started pulsing and glowing a beautiful golden colour. Matu focused on the magic lessons with Mrs Saito, and before he knew it, waves and waves of different spells flooded his mind. They came in such numbers and in such chaos that Matu had difficulty making them out as individual spells. He tried to focus on what he wanted for the door, and suddenly one single spell stood out brightly amongst all the others. Quickly, he placed his hand on the door and spoke the words to the spell before it vanished from his mind.

When he was finished, Matu opened his eyes. The second Band on his wrist vanished immediately, and all the spells disappeared from his mind in a whoosh. Matu looked at the door. For a moment it looked like the door rippled, as if made of liquid instead of solid wood. The next moment it looked like part of the door had vanished completely. As if there was a giant hole in it. Only the edges of the door were still there.

The rest of the door had gone, and Matu could see right into the empty corridor beyond.

Lian stood up in alarm. "What the hell did you do?"

Matu looked back at him, just as unnerved as Lian. He then turned and tried to open the door with the handle, just visible beside the open hole, before remembering that only Lian had the power to unlock it. Matu gestured to Lian, who opened the door for him. Matu stepped outside and closed the door behind him. From this side, the door looked exactly like it had done a few minutes earlier: completely intact and solid. He couldn't see through it.

"Can you still see me?" he called out to Lian.

"Yes, I can see you!" came Lian's voice from the other side.

Matu reached for the door handle again and slipped back inside, closing it behind him. "That magic Sophie has is extremely useful."

Lian stared at his brother. "Did you just do what I think you did?"

"We can see out, but they can't see in," Matu said proudly.

"That's disturbing," Lian muttered.

"At least we can see them coming now."

Lian sighed and closed his eyes, locking the door again. Matu looked back at the door. Lian was right, it was disturbing. The hole looked a little too real; like you could just walk right through it.

Matu walked over to the table. Nathan was sleeping as soundly as ever on top of it. His breathing was deep and slow. He was healing. However fast, Matu didn't know.

Matu sat back down beside Lian.

"There is nothing more we can do now, is there?" Lian asked.

It was a rhetorical question, but Matu answered anyway.

"Nope... Now all we can do is wait."

Chapter 5

Even without Mitrik with them, Sophie and Sky could do nothing in terms of escape. The bonds around their wrists had tightened ever since they left Mitrik, and that same white light was now also tied around their ankles so that they could do nothing more than shuffle along.

Kali didn't bother to lead them through thousands of passages in an attempt to confuse them enough to lose their bearings. She led them straight down three flights of narrow stairs and down a long corridor, before opening an iron door at the end. Perhaps she didn't think an escape was even possible.

Or maybe her arrogant King didn't think so.

Sophie hoped for the latter.

The iron door opened up into a long corridor with more doors on each side. Kali led the two of them into the corridor. At that point, Mitrik's second-in-command turned his head in response to a call from behind him. He checked back briefly with Mitrik's Third, presumably to make sure she could continue without him. She nodded curtly, and he left at a jog.

Kali held a hand firmly on the hilt of her dagger as she indicated that Sophie and Sky should move ahead of her, down the corridor. About halfway down, they came to a door on their right.

"In here," she directed, opening it. She ushered them through. Sophie eyed the two whips curled around each of Kali's shoulders as she passed.

It was unusual for even inner circle Disciples to have a signature weapon. Another feature that made this Disciple stand out more than any other. Sophie looked up at Mitrik's third-in-command and asked, "Your name is Kali?"

Kali stared at Sophie with her stone-cold look and said nothing. Once Sophie was inside, Kali reached for the door handle and started to pull it closed. Before she could do so completely, however, Mitrik's second-in-command re-appeared at her side, puffing slightly from his exertions.

"What?" she asked him coldly.

The second-in-command glanced at Sophie and Sky, who stood together a few feet away. After deeming them no threat, he leaned towards Kali and whispered something in her ear. Kali listened intently. Sophie tried to hear what the second-in-command was saying, but he was talking too softly. He also had a hand in front of his mouth, so she had no way of reading his lips.

Sophie glanced at Sky for a moment. He seemed just as confused as she was about the King's second and third-in-command discussing something right in front of them. Was this their way of portraying how much control they had over the situation? Arrogance seemed to run in Mitrik's higher ranks, too.

"Alone?" Kali snapped suddenly.

The second-in-command nodded. There was something in his eyes... anger? Fear?

"How long?" Kali asked. The man shook his head. He didn't know.

"You need to go with him," Kali said. Mitrik's Second nodded again. He then stared at Kali for a long moment, waiting for something. He glanced at Sky and Sophie again. Was that worry in his eyes?

"I'll be fine," Kali snapped.

The second-in-command looked at Kali once more. Then he walked smartly away.

Without another glance in their direction, Kali closed the iron door.

Sophie heard a lock click, and footsteps disappearing down the corridor.

They were alone.

"What the hell was that all about?" Sky muttered.

"No idea," Sophie said, shaking her head. In the distance she heard another door close. A few moments later the burning pressure around her wrists vanished. Sophie looked down and found that the white bonds of Mitrik's magic had disappeared. She spread her arms out and took one large step. All of Mitrik's magic around her had gone. She could move freely. She even felt her magic flow through her body again.

"You know you look really stupid when you do that," Sky grinned.

Sophie glared at him. She pulled her feet back together and dropped her arms to her side. Before she could say anything to her brother, Sky had turned serious and walked back to the iron door.

"We need to find a way out of here," he said. He studied the sides of the door, first looking up and then crouching down.

"Sky," Sophie started.

"Don't 'Sky' me," he snapped. "We need to get out! Do you have a plan? Tell me you have a plan."

"I don't have a plan," Sophie admitted.

Sky still didn't look at her. He jumped up from his crouch and tried the door handle. The door didn't budge. Sophie took a deep breath and kept herself from saying the first thing that came to mind. She knew he was trying to keep from panicking. He was the one who had heard Lian's voice calling for help. But there was no way that door handle was going to get them out.

"Then help me! We need to get out of here; we need to find Lian!" Sky shouted. He threw his body against the door. It wouldn't budge.

"Dammit, dammit!" Sky cursed.

Sophie rushed forward. "Sky, stop it."

"If I can just find its weak spot, it might work. I just have to—"

"It won't work," Sophie said. She placed a hand on Sky's shoulder.

He stilled at her touch for a moment, but then he stepped back from her.

"Why aren't you freaking out more? Lian needs us! And we're trapped here. He might be dying and we can't get to him!" He closed his eyes and raked his fingers through his dirty blonde hair.

"Look at me," Sophie started. Sky shook his head vigorously. Sophie placed her hands on his shoulders. He flinched at her touch but he didn't move away. "Look at me," she repeated, stronger now.

Sky swallowed, and opened his eyes.

"Your panicking will help Lian even less. You won't think rationally, and that will screw up our one chance of getting out of here. And believe me, when we figure out a way, we will only have one shot at getting it right."

Sky stared at her. He was hanging on to every word she was saying.

"When will that chance come?" he asked softly.

"I don't know," Sophie answered honestly.

"But Lian needs us now."

"I know. But he can't get to us now."

Sky closed his eyes for a moment.

"There is a reason Asters can use each other's powers," Sophie added. "Why we can use each other's blood. It's for moments like these. Lian has your blood; he can shimmer. Matu and Nathan have vials with blood from all of us. They know how to find a way to survive without us—without your shimmer and without my healing. Just like we need to find a way out of here without Matu's strength to bash through that door. We have to trust that they'll be all right. That Lian will be all right. And we need to focus on getting out of here. But you have to make peace with the fact that it could take a while."

"A while?"

"Maybe a day. Or longer."

"Lian doesn't have a day."

"We have to trust our brothers. If you don't, we might as well give up now."

Sky opened his eyes. The panic there seemed to have dissipated. There was a calm there now. A focus.

"I don't give up," he said.

The corner of Sophie's mouth twitched up into a tiny smile. She knew she'd said the words he needed to hear to get him to focus. She let go of his shoulders. "I know you don't."

There was something in the way Sky looked at her that Sophie couldn't quite place. "What?" she asked.

"I thought you were supposed to be the irrational, panicky one these days."

Sophie sighed in exasperation. "One! One minor lapse in judgment and you're going to hold it against me for the rest of my life."

Sky pulled up his right shoulder where a moment before Sophie's left hand rested. "Hard not to when I could literally *feel* your scars."

Sophie narrowed her eyes at her brother and pushed him away from her. "A 'thank you' would suffice."

Sky chuckled, but didn't thank her. Instead, he looked away from her and at the door. "Even if we did have access to Matu's blood, I don't think it would work."

"It might have done," Sophie said. She stepped closer to him and placed a hand on the cut at his throat.

"I don't think—"

"Will you shut up?" she hissed. She purposefully pressed her hand harder against the cut so he winced. He might've been right, but Sophie was testing a theory. She let her magic flow through her body. Her wrist started to tingle and her Band glowed a beautiful gold. Sophie could feel the magic course through her, down her arm and into the tips of her fingers. When the magic faded away, she removed her hand from Sky's throat. The cut had vanished. Not even a slim scar remained.

"Just what I thought," Sophie murmured. "It's just like the veil

45

outside. We can use magic within it. We just can't use it to get out."

"Well, I should hope so."

Sophie frowned at her brother.

Sky shrugged. "Mitrik would be a real idiot if we could just shimmer out right now."

"He does sound like an idiot."

"No arguments here."

"Pity, though. Would've made our escape so much easier," Sophie said.

Sky turned to his sister. "Have you thought of something?"

"Not yet," Sophie mused. She looked away from Sky long enough to really take in the room for the first time, and found herself surprised at what was there. "What the hell..."

The dungeon was nothing like the prison cells in the South American Underworld. Those were nothing more than small inlets cut into the rock, with a set of iron bars to keep the prisoners in. This dungeon was roomy. There were no windows, but multiple lanterns hung on the walls. There were two lounge chairs near a low coffee table, and on a low platform stood a double four-poster bed with four sets of plump, velvet cushions.

Sky also looked around the room. "He really does have a sense of humour."

"It's all an ironic joke," Sophie muttered. "Just like that woman's name."

"Yes, please do tell me why, while I was panicking about Lian, *you* were interested in her name?" Sky said sarcastically.

"Kali is the Hindi name of the warrior goddess of destruction," Sophie explained absently as she looked around the room. Sky watched her with a look of confusion.

"And that matters *because*...?"

"Queen Aiyana was named in Hindi. *Bhediya* means wolf. It's just ironic that his third-in-command has a Hindi name, when clearly she's not Hindu."

"I still don't see why it's relevant."

"I'm just saying. Mitrik might act like an idiot, and he might be way out of his depth to try and reclaim the Surface, *especially* with his re-opening of the fighting rings and drawing attention to himself. But he has his reasons. Nothing is random; not where they took the human hikers, not when he rang the alarm when he knew long before that we were there, none of it. It wouldn't surprise me that having a non-Hindu have a Hindi name means something, too. Didn't you think there was something about her?"

"She felt stronger than any Disciple I've ever met, but nothing more," Sky replied. He walked over to the bed and threw himself onto it. He scooted himself up and leaned against the headboard.

"There doesn't need to be more," Sophie said. "She is still stronger than any other Disciple. And faster. We don't have to worry about getting past Mitrik; we only need to worry about getting past *her*."

"Because Mitrik is leaving," Sky commented.

So he, too, understood the same thing she had, from the brief conversation Kali had with Mitrik's second-in-command.

"Right," Sophie agreed. She started pacing through the room, thinking. They knew that Mitrik was leaving, and that he had planned to leave alone. Kali wouldn't have had such a strong reaction to just anyone leaving alone, so it had to be her King, and it had to be somewhere Kali thought was dangerous enough that going alone wouldn't be smart. The second-in-command didn't know how long the King would be gone for, but he and Kali agreed he'd have to go with Mitrik. For protection? Or to convince the King to come back? Neither Kali nor the second-in-command thought that wherever the King was going was a good idea.

"Yes, I know all of that. I was there," Sky said irritably.

Sophie stopped her pacing. She hadn't realised she'd been speaking her thoughts out loud.

"By the way, the second-in-command is called Dan," Sky added.

Sophie stared at her brother incredulously. "Dan?"

"Yeah." Sky grinned. "It's shorter than *second-in-command*. Hearing you say that every time is getting on my nerves."

"Dan isn't very evil-sounding," Sophie pointed out.

Sky rolled his eyes. "Well, maybe you know a Hindu name for him? Would that make you feel better?"

"You mean Hindi."

"What?"

"Hindu is a person who practices the religion. Hindi is the language. You said Hindu, but you meant Hindi."

Sky rolled his eyes. "Could you please turn off the Sherlock switch for one second? Nobody cares."

"A Hindu might," Sophie pointed out.

Sky threw his hands up in the air in exasperation but said nothing.

Sophie cocked her head to the side and thought for a moment. "We could call him Archis?"

"What?"

"A Hindi name for Mitrik's second-in-command."

"I *can't* believe you actually know another Hindi name," Sky muttered. Sophie noted the slight concentration that Sky needed to say it right, but decided not to mention it.

"It means *ray of light*."

The two of them stared at each other for a moment, before bursting out laughing. It was a necessary release of stress, after the hours of tension since they began their mission.

Their moment of hilarity didn't last long, though. When the laughter stopped, they were once again reminded of where they were. Even though they had accepted they couldn't get to Lian any time quickly, that didn't mean they didn't need to plan an escape that would get them out of there as quickly as possible.

Sky jumped off the four-poster bed and started studying the space around it. "So... Might there be a way out of here?"

It didn't seem likely. Sophie thought for a moment. There was something else that didn't sit quite right with her. "Why would he keep us alive?" Sophie wondered aloud. Why give them the chance to escape?

Sky was on his knees now, studying whatever was underneath the four-poster, double bed. "He might want to use us in the fighting rings. Something like what Astaroth used to do with his maze," he offered.

Though Astaroth was the most powerful and famous King, until their parents killed him in the war twenty-five years ago, Sophie was still impressed Sky had remembered something about him from history class.

She shook her head. "No, he had the human hikers for that."

"He might've just used those hikers to draw us in."

"He didn't need the hikers to be used in the rings for that. Capturing them would've been enough. No, the humans were for the rings, which means we are for something else. He said he needed us to achieve his dream of freedom and seeing the ocean."

"Didn't that sound to you a little too..." Sky's voice was muffled by him being hidden half beneath the bed.

"Human?" Sophie offered.

"Yeah."

"He still needs to claim the Surface for it, though."

Sky's head popped up from beneath the bed. "That sounds more like a King. Though, it's not exactly comforting."

"He said he had big plans," Sophie continued.

Sky turned his attention to the back of the bed. "You have mind-reading in that knowledge skillset of yours? Would be helpful for knowing what he's up to."

"You know I don't," Sophie snapped.

"Shame," came Sky's voice from behind the headboard.

"You know you're not helping," Sophie grumbled. Only an arrogant arse like Sky could mock her magic right now.

Sophie wasn't fooled; she knew it was a defence mechanism for Sky at this moment. The fear of losing Lian was still there somewhere beneath the surface. It was within her, too, but she had to trust her other brothers. And her own knowledge, that a rash escape attempt would be worse in the long run.

"On the contrary. I think I'm helping quite a lot." He jumped up from behind the bed, his dark blue eyes shining brilliantly. He patted his hand on the headboard and said, "Help me move this."

"What?"

"Come on!" Sky grabbed the post on the left of the headboard and started pulling it back from the wall.

"You've got to be kidding me," Sophie muttered. She jumped up on the platform and pulled on the post on the right of the headboard. The bed was heavy, and it moved slowly, but it moved. Sophie looked down at the floor as they pulled the four-poster back inch by inch. And then she saw what Sky had found. A trapdoor revealed itself underneath the bed.

"He can't be this stupid," Sophie said.

"He might just be," Sky countered.

"Or it's a trap."

"It's a trapdoor, not a trap."

Sophie shot Sky a look, but he only grinned cockily back at her.

When the bed had been moved far enough away that all four edges of the trapdoor were out in the open, Sky knelt down and grabbed the handle. Sophie knelt down on the other side as she watched her brother pull. The door didn't budge.

"Come on," Sky grumbled. He interlaced his fingers and pulled hard again. The door gave way slightly. Sky groaned with effort and pulled again, and the trapdoor flew open. Sky stumbled backwards, but regained his balance. The door remained upright, perpendicular to the floor. Sky stepped up and peered over the edge of the trapdoor to see what was inside.

Sophie had already seen what was underneath.

"Dammit!" Sky shouted. He took the top of the trapdoor and threw it back down to the floor. It slammed shut with a bang.

"Like you said. He does have a sense of humour," Sophie said. For beneath the trapdoor was just stone flooring. No escape hatch, no tunnel, nothing. Just stone flooring, with white letters on it that spelled out *nice try*.

"He's insufferable!" Sky snapped. He stomped his foot on the ground and turned away from the trapdoor. Sophie couldn't help but chuckle at Sky's reaction to a prank he could've pulled himself, given half the chance.

Then something occurred to her.

Sky would've pulled the same prank.

"*You're* insufferable," Sophie repeated, a metaphorical lightbulb turning on in her head.

"That's very mature," Sky responded sharply.

"No, I'm serious," Sophie said, rising to her feet. "You're arrogant and find yourself totally amazing. It's the most annoying thing about you!"

Sky stared at his sister. "Okay, now you're just trying to make me feel bad for no reason."

"No, no, not for no reason. Mitrik—" Sophie pointed excitedly at the iron door, "—is arrogant, and finds himself totally amazing. He's insufferable and full of himself like you are. You are the closest thing we have to a brain that works like Mitrik's. And we need to figure out

51

what his plan is. So, if you were him, and you had two Asters in your dungeon, what would you do next?"

Sky had a look of absolute disbelief on his face. "You're seriously comparing me to *one of the Higher Kings of the Underworld*?"

"Yes! Now answer the question."

Sky stared at her.

"Come on!" Sophie insisted.

Sky rolled his eyes, but did seem to be thinking. "I would kill us. We're too big a threat if we'd manage to get out," he said eventually.

"But you don't believe we can get out. If the roles were reversed, and we had him here, bound to a chair, completely in our control... what would you do?"

"I'd kill him."

Sophie rolled her eyes. "That's too predictable," she scolded. "Think! If it was all up to you. If there were no rules or protocols you had to follow. If you could be your rash and arrogant self—" Sophie caught Sky's look and sighed, "—you know what, never mind. I hurt your pretty boy feelings and now you don't want to—"

"There is something I would do," Sky interrupted.

Sophie looked up at her brother. He was holding his hand out in front of him and was shaking his pointed finger up and down as he thought.

"I would still kill him. The history books tell enough stories of what can go wrong by leaving Kings alive. I wouldn't make that mistake," Sky said.

"Ironic that you are the one here remembering something from a history book," Sophie smirked.

"Would you stop it with the ironies? I'm actually trying to help you here," Sky snapped irritably.

"Sorry, sorry," Sophie said sarcastically. "I'll let your genius work in peace."

Sky rolled his eyes, but continued. "I would cut off his head and show it off to anyone who still deemed themselves better than me."

Sophie stared at her brother. "That's disturbing."

Sky shrugged. "You asked for it."

"Who would you even show it off to?"

"Your boyfriend, for a start."

Sophie sighed and looked away from Sky. "Well, I walked right into that one."

"Again, you asked for it," Sky replied lightly.

When Sophie turned back to him, she found Sky grinning at her. He was trying to make a joke of it, even though they both knew that he was very much speaking the truth.

"Who else?" Sophie asked.

Sky thought for a moment, but eventually said, "My mother."

Sophie's eyes widened. "Seriously? But she loves how strong you've become. Does she really see herself as better than you?"

"Not me specifically. Though she would love for me to be just like she was. But she never stops going on about how great her generation was. How flawlessly they worked together, and how they never needed to speak to know what the other would do, bla bla bla." Sky waved his hand. "She'll talk that way about us when I come back with a King's head on a platter."

Sophie let out a breath and shook her head. She knew Sky had a complicated relationship with his mother. A few years earlier they'd had a great falling out. Their relationship seemed to have almost returned back to the way it was before then. Though, that falling out had been around the same time that he'd started hiding away that kind and caring side of himself from anyone except for the Asters. And started sleeping with any girl willing, with no regard for their feelings, and with no plan to have anything more serious.

Sophie decided to keep her reaction airy and said, "All right then, we don't really have time to go into those kinds of issues right now. Though

I recommend a therapy session with Doctor Masalis when we get back."

"Just shut up, I was trying to help."

"You did," Sophie said, grinning. Finally, something Mitrik was doing was becoming clear. "There are only six people in the world who could possibly deem themselves better than Mitrik: the six other Kings. Aside from the South American King, Mitrik is the youngest, and after what the South American one did to Gayle—" Sophie closed her eyes for a second, swallowed, and then continued. "Mitrik will be seen as the baby of the bunch."

"Baby or not, he won't be stupid enough to show us off to all of them," Sky said. He sat back down on the four-poster bed and leaned back on his hands.

"Right. So, he will choose one in particular. Like he said himself, he's not a fighter. He knows he cannot claim the Surface by himself. He needs an alliance."

Sky lifted his head at that. "That hasn't happened since the original seven Kings."

"Not a complete alliance of all seven Kings, no," Sophie said.

"Or any alliance. They're all too proud and angry to ask for help. And they don't trust any of the others because they're not brothers by blood like the original seven were. So why would Mitrik try?" Sky replied.

"Because he's heard too many stories to try and take the Surface by himself. He might not trust any of the other Kings, but he needs one, maybe two, to try and achieve his dream." Sophie placed both hands on her hips and looked around the room. "So, which of the other six would he choose to start with?"

"Kirnon?" Sky offered. "He's the only original King left. He's ancient and powerful. And with my wit and skill we'd make one hell of a team."

Sophie groaned at her brother's imitation of Mitrik. He gave her another one of his grins. "But Kirnon hasn't moved in centuries. The Asian Underworld is practically a ghost town. There's barely any

Disciples left there. They all bailed after the war Astaroth waged against our parents."

Kirnon was out. Sophie's mind raced as everything she knew about every King flashed through her mind. She weighed the odds; she looked at what each King had done in the past, what their powers were, and which one would be the safest bet to start an alliance with. Which one of them was powerful, but not so powerful as to think they didn't need what Mitrik offered? Which one did need what Mitrik offered, but wasn't a liability?

Names swirled in her mind, but Sophie kept coming back to the same one. She paused her pacing and looked at her brother.

Sky immediately read the expression on her face. "You know, don't you?"

"There is only one... Only one who hasn't shown their hand yet. Who hasn't yet attempted to attack the Surface at all. One who has proven to be powerful, but very subtle and smart. One who didn't use armies and weapons, but tactics and misdirection to achieve his goal, and who was the only one ever to fully achieve his goal before vanishing once again. One we know almost nothing about. What's a more strategic alliance than one with the King the Asters don't know?"

Sky tipped his head back as every word Sophie spoke sunk in. "He's going after the King who killed the Queen."

Sophie nodded slowly. "Yep... The King who killed the Queen."

Sky dropped onto his back on the bed and stared at the ceiling, sighing heavily. "If that alliance happens, we are so, *so* screwed."

Chapter 6

For a moment Axel just stared at the screen.

Lian was alive. Axel didn't know how, but he was.

Matu and Nathan had also vanished from the Surface. Axel couldn't track their locations anymore either. They were somewhere in the Underworld. Axel assumed they were the ones to get to Lian in time.

Nathan's image was quite a bit darker than the other four, but Axel wasn't worried. On the computer, Axel could look into the Aster's well-being in further detail. Nathan was just exhausted, utterly exhausted. But he was alive, too. And his heart rate had slowed, which meant he was getting his rest. Lian and Matu's heart rates were normal as well. The three of them didn't seem to be in any danger.

Axel had full confidence that the Asters would continue with their mission, and do it well. It almost never happened that the Asters were sent in, ran into no trouble at all, finished a job, and were back on Saluverus within two days. Axel hadn't expected anything like that this time either. But as long as all the Asters were still all right, and they were managing to get enough rest throughout their mission, they would be fine.

They would finish the job.

They were trained well.

"He's fine," Nicholas said. His shift of watching the Asters had started fifteen minutes ago, but Axel had refused to leave the Board Room until he knew for sure that Lian was all right. He supposed he could leave Nicholas to it now. At this moment, there was nothing the Small Council needed to do.

Axel let out a long breath. "I'll leave you, then," he said. He placed both hands on the armrests and pushed himself up out of his chair. He headed to the door.

Axel didn't even have his hand on the door handle when Nicholas gasped and called, "Axel!"

Axel spun around and stared at the screen, heart pounding in his chest. It couldn't possibly go wrong so quickly, could it?

But when he looked up at the television screen, all five Aster images were unchanged. Four were shining brightly, while Nathan's was still slightly darker due to his exhaustion. But the images were the same.

Then why...

"It's Diallo," Nicholas said. Axel followed Nicholas' pointed finger to the computer screen. Axel's heart leapt to his throat.

Something was very, very wrong.

Diallo's image wasn't darkening, as if close to death. But it was flickering wildly. Axel had never seen anything like it before in all his working life as Ambassador.

It kept flickering faster and faster.

"Call Madeleine, NOW!" Axel ordered.

But it wasn't necessary. On the left screen they saw the map of Brazil, zoomed in on the area where Diallo had set up his final encampment before his departure back to Saluverus with his research team. There were two bright blue spots on the camp; Madeleine was already there.

Axel was halfway through letting out a breath of relief when he registered that there were a number of black dots in the same vicinity. Disciples had suddenly appeared at the camp.

And then, Diallo's image went completely dark.

Madeleine had barely heard Diallo's call. It was no more than a croak, hardly even her name, but she'd heard it nonetheless. She was right in the middle of carrying a sofa up the stairs to her friend Orla's new living room, when it came. The distress in Diallo's voice was enough to stop her in her tracks. She dropped her side of the sofa, and only managed a curt apology to Orla before she shimmered out.

She followed the sound of Diallo's groan. Why he couldn't even properly enunciate her name sent a spike of worry through her, as her shimmer swept her away from Sydney, Australia, and to the dense jungles of Brazil.

When she arrived, her feelings didn't improve. Instead, she was faced with one of her worst nightmares.

She had appeared in the middle of Diallo's camp; more specifically in one of the sleeping tents. And right in front of her, sitting upright in his hammock, was Diallo. Except he wasn't sitting up of his own accord. A Disciple was holding him up, and had a knife at his throat.

Madeleine looked at Diallo, trying to meet his gaze. But Diallo's eyes were droopy when the Disciple cut his throat.

"NO!" Madeleine screamed.

A blind rage descended upon her. She didn't care that she had no weapons and wasn't exactly wearing fighting gear. Before she knew it, she used her magic of Speed and Flight and charged straight at the Disciple. He didn't know what hit him. He was on his back, with her on top of him a second later. He dropped the knife on impact. Madeleine gave him one hard whack of her fist against the side of his head before jumping off and snatching up the knife.

Another moment later she buried the knife in the Disciple's chest. And again and again. The image of Diallo's eyes as his throat was slit was so bright in her mind's eye. She stabbed the Disciple another two times. She might have kept going if there hadn't been a scream behind her.

And then reality set in around her.

The whole camp echoed with screaming. Madeleine got up from her dead Disciple and looked around. In the other tent rooms a few lights flickered, and Madeleine could see shadows running around. And she could hear the shouts of the attackers, and the screams of the victims.

But even as Madeleine registered the screams, they were already dying out. Shadows still moved around, though.

With the Disciple's knife in her hand, Madeleine dug into her magic and sped through the tent and out into the camp site. Even with only her single knife the Disciples didn't stand a chance. They didn't see her coming, and by the time they did, they were already dead. She was too fast, too deadly, too angry.

Madeleine breathed heavily. Her hands were shaking as she took in her surroundings. There was blood on her clothes and in her hair. Her hands were sticky with it.

Fifteen Disciples were dead around her. Her work was messy; all done out of rage. But none of them got even a scratch on her.

There were Affinites, too. Innocent Affinites, who were just there to find out what happened to Gayle Mendosa; how she died. And now they were dead. All five of them.

Madeleine stilled.

Five.

No, she was supposed to pick up seven tomorrow. She was going to shimmer seven Affinites back tomorrow. Seven Affinites and Diallo.

Without another thought, Madeleine dug into her magic and flew through the camp. And over it. And through the surrounding area.

Two might have got away. Two might still be alive.

If only Madeleine could find them.

They could tell her why Diallo didn't fight back. Why he had that glassy look in his eyes and could be held up by a Disciple without any resistance. What the hell happened to him?

In her short search of the perimeter, she couldn't find anyone. Madeleine widened her search and flew around the camp again.

All she could do was fly around. She made sure the blue light of her shimmer was visible as she flew. If any Affinite saw it, they would know it was her. They would know they were safe.

But then again, they'd had Diallo with them. And they hadn't been safe with him. He didn't protect them.

The Ceder of Strength couldn't protect them.

Madeleine felt her heart break as she saw his death over and over again in the back of her mind, as she flew around.

For five, ten, fifteen minutes she scoured the area. There were no Affinites to be found. She couldn't see anyone anywhere. The jungle was utterly silent.

In the darkness, and with her blue light making her a perfect target, Madeleine knew she should be more careful, but she no longer cared. She didn't care if there were any Disciples left with a crossbow or a bow and arrow, to shoot her out of the sky. Have them take their best shot, she thought. Let them try.

But no bolt nor arrow ever came.

Silence reigned in the darkened jungle.

Madeleine circled the camp once more, before returning to the sleeping tent. There she stood, motionless, as she stared at Diallo's lifeless form. His whole body was covered in the blood that had spurted from his cut throat. His eyes were still open, but Madeleine couldn't move to close them.

She stared at him.

And then for a while longer.

It was like she could feel her heart being ripped into a million pieces.

Then she let out a cry and dropped to her knees.

With a sip of Madeleine's blood, Rose and Katherine appeared in Brazil. They found Madeleine kneeling in front of Diallo's body.

Katherine's breath hitched when she saw him. Even from here, she could see there was nothing more she could do. The second that blade was pulled along his throat, Diallo was dead. There was no way she could've got here fast enough to heal him. To save him.

Madeleine looked horrible as well. She'd shimmered here right from Sydney. She was wearing sandals, dark, three-quarter-length trousers and what used to be quite a nice blouse. Now, everything was covered in blood.

She was bent over on her knees and had her arms wrapped tightly around herself. She was rocking back and forth slowly, and sobbing.

"Maddie..." Rose whispered. She stepped towards Madeleine, and knelt down beside her. She wrapped an arm around her.

Katherine walked over to Diallo's body. The sight of him was absolutely unbelievable. The strength Katherine knew this man to have... To see him lying like this, that a single attack had killed him.

"Do you know what happened?" Rose asked Madeleine softly.

Katherine looked up to see Madeleine's reaction. Madeleine stopped her rocking and opened her eyes.

"He didn't even move," she ground out. Her voice was hoarse. Her eyes were red and swollen, but she'd stopped crying. "He was held by one man. He didn't even fight back when they... when they cut his throat."

Katherine stared at Madeleine.

She'd seen it happen.

She'd been only a few seconds too late. Diallo had called her only a few seconds too late.

Katherine looked down at the man she considered to be part of her family. The last male Ceder, gone as well.

For a moment, Katherine closed her eyes. She forced her emotions to the back of her mind; made sure she could think practically now. When she opened her eyes, the first thing she did was look around the tent. Her eyes found a thin, brown scarf amongst other pieces of clothing thrown on a chair nearby. Katherine took it from the back of a chair and placed it over Diallo's exposed throat. She lifted his head and wrapped the scarf around his neck. He might still be covered in his own blood, but at least the wound wasn't so visible.

"Why wouldn't he fight?" Rose asked.

Katherine couldn't look at her; couldn't look at Madeleine. She stared at the brown scarf she'd just wrapped around Diallo's neck. Something didn't make sense. There was only one reason why Diallo wouldn't fight.

"Because he couldn't," Katherine thought out loud, still not looking at either Rose or Madeleine.

"That doesn't make any sense..." Rose started. "How would that happen?"

"I don't know," Katherine whispered.

"But *how*? This is Diallo we're talking about. How could something just happen that could cause him to—"

"I said *I don't know*!" Katherine shouted. She held her head with her hands and dug her nails into the skin on her head. She barely registered the pain of it.

Rose physically recoiled at Katherine's outburst. Katherine regretted it immediately. But she couldn't handle Rose's questions. Not now. Not with Diallo lying there in front of them. Not with the smell of decaying bodies filling the humid air around them. Katherine couldn't keep her emotions under control while being bombarded with questions that she didn't have the answers to. Her magic of Health and Knowledge couldn't help her with that. She couldn't just magically detect the reason Diallo didn't fight. The only thing she could think of, was that there was a physiological reason why Diallo *couldn't* fight back.

But Katherine chose not to say that right now. A comment like that would raise more questions than answers. It was up to Saluverus' pathologists to figure out what had caused Diallo's death. Not the knife across his throat, but the circumstances leading up to that.

There had to be a reason. Katherine had to believe that. She did believe it. She couldn't think of any other possibility for why this had happened.

"There are still two out there," Madeleine muttered.

Katherine dropped her hands immediately. She stepped closer to Madeleine and Rose and looked around, as if expecting a Disciple to jump out and attack them at any second.

"Affinites..." Madeleine corrected. "I meant Affinites. There are only five here. I was supposed to shimmer back seven tomorrow."

"You flew around? You couldn't find them?" Rose asked.

Madeleine's silence was answer enough.

"Well, you were alone. And distraught," Rose said, rubbing Madeleine's arm. "We will find them. With my connection to the nature around here, we should have a better chance. Kat and I worked with some great researchers on our team. We can assemble a very specific—"

"NO," Madeleine snapped. Then she added softer, but equally

determined, "No... no more teams. No more Affinites." Madeleine brushed off Rose's hand and rose to her feet. Her tears had dried. Her eyes were still red, but they were filled with fiery determination. Katherine had only ever seen such conviction in Madeleine once before. It sent chills down her spine.

"No more Affinites. No Affinite will be sent in to do an Aster's job—a Ceder's job. No... We will find those two who are still missing, and then we will leave this godforsaken place. This King already took so many Affinites. He took Cara and Tomas, and now Diallo, as well...... And he took Gayle."

The three Ceders stared at each other. The enormity of these combined losses weighed heavily between them. They were the last three of seven Ceders standing.

"No one else is dying here," Madeleine added eventually. "I will make sure of it, *if it is the last thing I do.*"

Chapter 7

It was early afternoon when Jillian Kelly trudged wearily from Saluverus' village centre to the Medical Bay. The glass doors slid open and, after she stepped inside, she turned left and headed slowly towards the trauma ward.

Jillian had visited her father many times since he'd come back from Brazil. She'd sat at his bedside while he slept. She tried talking to him in the moments he was awake, but he never seemed to be able to talk back. There was always something in his eyes that told her that he recognised her, and knew what she was saying, but something was preventing him from forming a single sentence to reply properly.

Her father was always calm when Jillian arrived for her visits. She had heard about the shocking fight he had put up when Sky shimmered him here, and when Sophie and Katherine tried to heal him. And about his jumbled words when he did speak. Jillian didn't know what to think herself; though she barely thought at all lately. Every time she thought, she thought about her dead mother. And if she didn't want to think about that, her mutilated and traumatised father came to mind instead.

Sylvia Allen and her uncle, Jackson, had asked her last night to try and coax her father into speaking about his experiences in Brazil. Reluctantly she had agreed, but the moment Jillian brought up the Amazon Rainforest, her father unleashed a ramble of words that no one understood; then he started to panic and pull apart his bandages.

And he was still so fragile. He was still so broken. Every panic attack he had, risked so much damage; he might still not survive this whole thing.

Jillian moved slowly through the Medical Bay corridors. This wasn't what she thought her life would be like. After Gayle had died, which had been heart breaking at the time, Jillian had expected her family to be permanently reunited on Saluverus. But no sooner had her father come back, than her mother left. And when her father lost contact with her mother, he'd left again to go after her.

Neither came back.

Jillian hadn't thought that when Axel had come to find her, that he'd come with the news that her mother was found dead, and that her father was in the midst of an emergency operation.

She'd thought she'd still have her father. That they could pull each other through their grief at the loss of her mother.

Nothing could be less true.

Her father was broken, mentally and physically. Whatever had happened to him in the Amazon, had demolished all the structures that had made him such a tough and resilient Affinite, and left him stuck in a place worse than death.

There had been one moment, the day before, when Jillian had talked to him about her mother, about the pain she felt at her being gone. Her father had listened. He looked at her and for a brief moment Jillian would see the sadness in his eyes. That look was enough to make her heart break all over again. And soon that sadness got taken over by more panic and a string of nonsensical words.

Jillian didn't expect today to be much different. Except that she wasn't going to talk about her mother again. And she wasn't going to bring up the Amazon again. Jillian wasn't even sure she could bear to look at her father in the state he was in. Each time she came only hurt her more. There was this hollow ache inside her chest that grew with every passing day.

Her father had been moved from intensive care to the trauma ward when Bianka Mazur had deemed him recovered enough from his physical injuries. He was now in a room that had a large rectangular window on the corridor side. It was one-way glass.

Jillian walked past the nurse's station and headed for the glass window. Jackson and Arthur were already there. They greeted Jillian as she approached, and each hugged her tight. She didn't hug them back. Pretending to be glad to see them took energy that she didn't have. She disentangled herself quickly from them and stood in between her uncle and cousin, and looked through the glass.

Psychotherapist, Olga Masalis, was sitting in a chair beside her father's bed. Sylvia Allen was standing at the foot of the bed, talking to Olga and a man that Jillian had never seen before. He was tall and skinny and wearing a scruffy, plain grey suit. His brown hair was cut short and his face was bony and stern-looking.

"Who's he?" Jillian asked, unable to keep the exhaustion from her voice.

"Arnar Jakobsson," Jackson replied. "He's the speech therapist from Iceland. Olga thought speaking in Icelandic would help your father feel more comfortable."

Jillian stared through the glass. Her father and uncle were half-Icelandic, but considered themselves completely Icelandic. Their surname didn't suggest it because their father had been Saluverian, which meant that his ancestors had lived on Saluverus ever since the Original War. Jillian's grandmother was from Iceland, and her father and uncle had been brought up there until their fighting skills had become so abundantly clear that they were asked to move to Saluverus to train with the Asters.

This was the first time Jillian had actually seen the speech therapist. She knew he'd arrived two days ago, and had already worked with her father at least once.

Jillian saw Sylvia nod once and walk out of the room. She deliberately closed the door behind her and then looked at the three of them standing in front of the window; her expression was sombre.

"Jillian, how are you doing?" the Consul asked.

Jillian didn't reply; didn't even look at Sylvia.

Sylvia cleared her throat. "There is no change. He speaks the same way in Icelandic as he does in English."

Jillian could see her father in the hospital bed. The head of the bed had been brought up, and with the help of a few pillows he was sitting upright. He was looking back and forth between Olga and Arnar with a look of distrust.

"What does Olga say?" Jackson asked.

"She said she wanted Jakobsson to have three sessions before making her assessment," Sylvia answered. She took a place beside Jackson and looked through the glass, as well. "This is the third."

"How are his injuries?" Arthur asked from Jackson's other side.

"Healing well. Bianka did an outstanding job. She came in this morning for a check-up and thinks he will recover without any loss of mobility."

"Good..." Arthur said, rubbing Jillian's arm. "That's good, Jill."

Jillian attempted to nod and smile, but it was hard pretending to be glad about something she didn't care about. Mobility was not even near the top of her list of worries when it came to her father's recovery. She just wanted her father back; the man she knew him to be. Take away the soldier, there was still a man underneath. Jillian couldn't see that man anywhere within the shell that was lying in the hospital bed on the other side of that glass.

Jillian hunched her shoulders and dropped her head. She couldn't help the tears that started running down her cheeks.

Arthur wrapped his arm around her shoulders and held her tightly.

Jillian didn't move away from his embrace this time. She rested her head against his shoulder.

From that angle, she watched as her father's eyes darted from Olga to Arnar Jakobsson. In some ways this was worse than him dying in the Amazon Rainforest like her mother. In some ways her father was as dead as she was. Everything that made him who he was, certainly seemed to be gone.

Her father's eyes continued to snap from the speech therapist to the psychotherapist and back again. Jillian saw that it was getting worse, and tensed within Arthur's arms. His hands by his side had started shaking and were clenching and unclenching. He was shaking his head slightly, his lips quivering.

"It's happening again," Jillian said quietly. She had seen this panic attack before. She'd been right next to him when it happened. Usually, he calmed down after a while, and he would turn to the ceiling and mumble sentences that didn't make sense; about darkness and light and bringing death and keeping away light.

But this time was different. This time he wasn't calming down; he was getting worse. Jillian saw his legs shaking and he was now bashing his fists onto the mattress by his sides.

Arnar Jakobsson stood up out of his chair and tried to hold down Percy's arms in an attempt to calm him down. Olga Masalis joined him.

But they were not just holding down any patient.

They were holding down a soldier. A disorientated, angry, delirious soldier, and neither the speech therapist, nor the psychotherapist, had a body built for fighting.

Jillian's father had started shouting now, and he managed to swing his legs over the side of the bed and throw Arnar Jakobsson off him and into the chair behind him. He then grabbed Olga by the collar and threw her across him to the ground on the other side of his bed. He was about to jump to his feet when Arnar pushed himself off the chair and tried again.

In a flash, Arthur let go of Jillian and turned to follow his father, who was already pulling the door open to get into the room. Unlike Olga and Arnar, Jackson and Arthur were born fighters.

Jillian remained motionless on the other side of the window. Some part of her willed her to be brave and go in and help. But she couldn't move; she couldn't get close to that again.

Sylvia moved to put her arm around Jillian. Jillian had put her hand over her mouth and watched how her uncle and her cousin advanced on her father. Before they got to him, Percy jumped off the bed and onto his feet. He screamed loudly as he landed on his still-recovering leg, and Jillian moved her hands to cover her ears to block out the piercing sound.

Jackson and Arthur were there a second later, and they took Percy by his shoulders and heaved him back onto the bed.

"NO! No leaving! Bringing dark death! Leaving keeps light! Light! No leaving! No!" Jillian's father shouted, as Jackson and Arthur held Percy's arms and chest strongly down against the mattress.

"Hold his legs still," Arthur told Arnar.

Jillian forced herself to watch as the three men gave her father absolutely no room to move. He continued to struggle; he continued to shout about light and death and darkness and bringing and leaving. He'd been saying those things ever since he'd regained consciousness.

Eventually, her father stopped struggling against the three sets of hands that were holding him down. His shouting turned to mumbling until, at last, he stopped talking completely. Jillian could see his eyes flutter and she could tell that he was losing consciousness. She felt numb, staring at this tormented stranger who was her father.

"Call Bianka!" Jackson called.

"Come on," Sylvia said, and with a gentle force in her hands, she guided Jillian away from the window. Losing sight of her father gave

Jillian that little extra energy. She and Sylvia headed quickly over to the nurse's station. Dagmara, the Polish nurse who had been on call the night her father had been brought in, was there. She had already moved around the station and looked at Jillian with a question in her eyes.

Sylvia nodded to the nurse urgently and said, "Bianka, yes."

Dagmara nodded and headed down the hall at speed. The Polish nurse had been transferred from the recovery ward to the trauma ward with Jillian's father. Since she had been the one who knew everything about Percy from the moment he had been brought in, it was decided to have her near him for all her shifts until he improved enough or could be moved out of the Medical Bay.

Jillian and Sylvia headed back to her father's room and found Arthur and Jackson standing outside with Olga Masalis and Arnar Jakobsson. Jillian glanced into the room and saw her father lying motionless in the hospital bed. His skin was a horrible grey colour, and he looked absolutely exhausted. A wave of anguish washed through Jillian as she came to stand next to her cousin.

Arthur immediately threw his arm around her. He had always been protective of her. Ever since news had come in about her parents, he'd barely left her side. Jillian tried to welcome his care when she could.

"Bianka is coming," Sylvia told Jackson.

Jackson nodded his approval.

"What did we miss?" Sylvia asked.

"They want to move him," Arthur told her.

Jillian moved her head towards the psychotherapist. "*Home?*"

Her parents' house was in the middle of the village on Saluverus. How was moving him there, where he could be a danger not just to himself, but to innocent Affinites so close around him, a good idea? Add to that being surrounded by memories of his recently passed wife?

"No, not back home," Olga Masalis said in her Greek accent. "We want to move him out of the Medical Bay to somewhere he knows and will be more comfortable. If he's more at rest and in a place he feels safe, his speech might recover, too."

"Where do you suggest he goes?" Jackson asked.

"It can't be near many other people. We don't want what happened today to happen to unwitting inhabitants of Saluverus. Perhaps there is somewhere like this in your ancestral home in Iceland?"

Iceland.

Jillian couldn't imagine her father going to Iceland. He'd barely spent any time there; most of his youth he'd lived on Saluverus, and for the last eighteen years he'd lived in Brazil. And she wouldn't be able to visit him. Even though the look of him pained her, she'd still want to see her father, even if he wasn't the father she remembered.

As if reading her thoughts, Arthur squeezed her arm in sympathy.

"He doesn't have anywhere to go back to in Iceland," Jackson said, putting Jillian's thoughts into words. He thought for a moment. "There may be a place on Saluverus that will work. We stayed there often as kids. But I need to be there every time you or a nurse goes in to help him, because that—" he pointed through the one-way glass "—cannot happen again if there is no one there to protect you. You were lucky we were here this time."

Olga nodded, but said, "You need to continue with your job, and we will continue with ours. We will have soldiers with us standing outside to make sure nothing happens to us or to your brother. We will arrange plans and prepare for his move. It should be as soon as possible. Would tomorrow be all right?"

Jackson nodded.

Jillian looked back through the glass. She had a vague idea of the place Jackson had in mind for her father. Yet she couldn't help wondering if her father would ever be able to speak normally again, even if he was in an environment that he felt comfortable in. From what Jillian could see, and from what she had learnt when she was at school about PTSD and other mental illnesses, she didn't have much hope that the father she had grown to know and love would ever truly come back.

Jillian swallowed. What on earth had the South American King done to him?

Chapter 8

Nathan awoke late the following afternoon. Matu and Lian hadn't had any trouble with Disciples trying to barge into the room. They'd used Sophie's magic again to cast one final spell. This one Lian had placed at the other end of the corridor. Neither Lian nor Matu knew exactly how the spell worked, but, from inside their room, they could now hear everything that happened at the end of the corridor. They could hear any Disciple that walked past, and any conversation that was held near it.

Sophie would be proud of them, wherever she was.

Maybe a little less proud when she found out they could only cast the spells because they used her magic of Knowledge, and not because they actually remembered the spells themselves.

Either way, the spells were extremely useful. It meant that Lian and Matu would know of any Disciple stepping into their side corridor, long before they'd reach the door. Luckily, no Disciple ever did.

During his nightshifts, Lian had sat in front of the door, looking through the one-way opening. He had lost count of how many Disciples had walked past their side corridor, unaware that three Asters were mere feet away from them. Only a King was able to sense their presence in his Underworld. Lian wondered why he hadn't raised the alarm yet. Though, he was glad Mitrik hadn't. He was also glad this room was rarely used. It gave Nathan the peace he needed to rest and heal completely, and it gave him and Matu the time to catch up on some much-needed sleep, too.

"How are you feeling?" Lian asked when Nathan finally stirred and propped himself up onto his elbows.

"Rested," Nathan replied. "How long was I out?"

"Almost twenty-four hours," Matu told him.

Nathan closed his eyes for a moment. The colour had returned to his skin. Lian still couldn't quite fathom what Nathan had managed to do the day before. Lian had been close to death before, but never that close. After he'd lost his vision, he vaguely remembered something tightening around him, but he hadn't been able to place the feeling. It was only after Matu had healed him, that he saw the vines and understood what had happened. How Nathan's magic could work over such distance, to wrap him up and keep him from bleeding out... Lian didn't want to think about what kind of miracle it was that he was still alive.

"What about Sophie and Sky? Any word?" Nathan asked. It was interesting to see how the cold of a mission wasn't part of Nathan yet. He was still waking up, and the worry for Sophie and Sky was clear. When they would go back into action, that worry would quickly disappear.

Both Lian and Matu shook their heads.

"Do we have any idea where they are?" Nathan asked.

"I couldn't reach Sky yesterday," Lian said. "I used his magic to track him as best I could, but it only got me this far before I fell. I called him but he didn't respond."

Matu looked sideways at him. "We did the same. They're somewhere where he can't hear us."

"You mean like another veil?" Lian asked.

"Possibly," Matu said. "We need to find out where they are."

"And now that you're back and awake—" Lian said as he patted Nathan on the leg, "—we can start doing that."

"One question," Nathan said slowly. "Why did you let me rest in a room that has a hole in the door?"

Both Lian and Matu turned to look at the door. They realised how strange it must seem to someone who hadn't been there when they cast the spell.

"And what do I hear?" Nathan asked before either of them could answer his first question.

Lian pricked up his ears and listened intently. Disciples were heading down the wider corridor. They were nearing the point where Lian had placed the spell. The Disciples were still quite far away, but Lian could just make out what they were saying because they were speaking loudly and excitedly.

"We led them right to him!" a male voice said.

"He'd better thank us for that—we made it so easy for him," another male, deeper voice said.

A female laugh. "Oh please, you got lucky."

The voices were getting closer.

"We *did not* get lucky," said a third, younger male voice.

The chatter continued, their footsteps slowing, apparently in no hurry.

"They know something," Nathan said.

Lian glanced over to his brother. As he suspected, the warmth had completely disappeared. Nathan was fully awake, and the frozen calm had descended upon him. Now only the task at hand was his focus.

"We need disguises," Matu said. "If Sophie and Sky are in real danger, we need to get close, unnoticed."

He didn't need to say any more for Nathan and Lian to understand. Nathan swung his legs to the side and jumped off the table. Lian was already at the door. He opened it and slipped into the side-corridor, Matu and Nathan close on his heels.

"Come on! You have to tell us!" the first male asked.

"Yeah, are the rumours true?" the younger male added.

"You know I can't tell you anything," the female replied. "Right, Seph?"

The third male grunted deeply.

The three Asters tiptoed to the end of the corridor, until they were just around the corner of the main hallway. Matu stood in front; he turned his head to look back at his brothers. His eyes said everything: the four Disciples had turned into the hallway and were getting closer by the second. "We keep them alive," he instructed in a whisper.

Both Lian and Nathan nodded.

They waited, coiled for action, as the footsteps came closer. The four Disciples continued to chat nonchalantly. When they reached the side-corridor, they were taken completely by surprise. They were still reaching for their weapons when Matu jumped out first and knocked two male Disciples out cold. When Nathan followed, he had a vine shoot from his hand and wrap around the neck of the third male Disciple. He tugged hard, pulling the Disciple forward so fast that he couldn't stay on his feet. He hit the ground hard. Lian focused his attention on the single female of the group. He had Sky's dagger at her throat before she could even free her sword from its sheath at her hip.

"In there," Matu ordered, gesturing to the room they had just come out of.

"You scream, you're dead, got it?" Lian whispered in the woman's ear as he guided her towards the door.

"Only cowards scream," she hissed. Lian wasn't sure if that made her brave or just an idiot. Behind him, Matu was dragging the two unconscious Disciples towards the room, and Nathan was doing the same with the one he knocked to the ground.

Nathan opened the door and they stepped inside. Lian guided the female Disciple to one of the chairs and pushed her down upon it. He looked quickly over his shoulder and saw that Matu had left the two Disciples he'd knocked unconscious just inside the door. The third male

Disciple that Nathan had pulled inside, was groaning and regaining consciousness.

"Nate," Lian said, still with Sky's dagger at the woman's throat.

Nathan looked up and the Band on his wrist began to glow. Green vines started growing from the ground around the chair. They snaked up the legs of the chair and bound the Disciple's ankles tightly to them. Other vines twisted up even further and wrapped themselves around her torso and the back of the chair. Only when Lian was certain that she couldn't move, did he pull the dagger away.

Over by the door, Matu was stripping the other two male Disciples of their weapons and laying them on the table in the middle of the room. Lian pulled around another chair and placed it next to the female Disciple. Nathan came over, pulling the third, half-conscious Disciple behind him. Lian helped put the Disciple on the chair, and moments later he, too, was bound to the chair with Nathan's vines. Lastly, Nathan turned his magic to the two unconscious Disciples by the door, wrapping them in vines also.

Lian looked at the weapons Matu had tossed on the table. Some of them were black with white lines in the hilt, while others were completely bone white. Lian stepped towards the woman to unbuckle her weapons belt. As he pulled it off, he saw that all her weapons were bone white as well, while the other bound Disciple only had black weapons.

Right then, Lian remembered part of the conversation they'd overheard.

Are the rumours true?

You know I can't tell you that.

She knew something more than the others. She was higher ranked than the others. Lian turned to face her. She had dark skin and short black hair. She had bulky shoulders and strong-looking arms.

"Where are our brother and sister?" he asked her.

Her dark brown eyes turned wicked as she said, "Dead."

Lian had interrogated enough Disciples to know that she was lying. Nothing was more fun for Disciples than to see the fear of a sibling's death in the eyes of an Aster. That fun was starting to get old.

"Don't lie to me," Lian snapped.

"They will be. He'll make a nice show of it," she said.

He.

Lian had a horrible feeling that he knew who the Disciple was talking about.

The Disciple next to her rolled his head around and blinked.

"Where are they now?" Matu asked from behind Lian.

"Oh, you must at least know that," the woman drawled scornfully.

Lian thought of what he knew about the North American King. Even though he never paid much attention in classes, he and Sky knew that, whenever a teacher started talking about a King, they needed to stop goofing around and listen. For North America, there was one place Lian knew for sure that Sky wouldn't be able to hear their call.

Nathan knew it, too. His cold voice filled the room as he said, "They're in the white castle."

It wasn't a question. Neither Disciple responded, but something flashed in the eyes of the male Disciple when the words were spoken, telling them all they needed to know. The woman was better trained, which was probably why she was higher ranked. Her hostile face revealed nothing.

"What is he keeping them alive for?" Matu asked them.

The woman shot a look at the Disciple next to her, before turning back to face Lian and Matu. She cocked her head to the side as her eyes turned sly. "The fighting rings?" she mused.

"The humans were for the rings," Nathan said. He was standing by the door, making sure no one was coming, while also keeping an eye on the other two Disciples still unconscious on the floor.

"Ah, so you know that already," she said in a bored tone.

"Answer the damn question," Matu snarled.

The Disciple just stared at the both of them. She knew what plans Mitrik had for Sophie and Sky, that much was clear. He was going to make a show of their deaths; the trio of Asters knew that much, too. But for who? And where? And when...

When she refused to answer, Lian turned his attention to the Disciple on her right. "What are the rumours?" he asked.

There was something still youthful in his demeanour, and Lian's question seemed to alight some sort of excitement within him. He wasn't yet properly trained in the art of keeping feelings and knowledge to himself. To portray nothing; reveal nothing.

"He's going to make a show of their deaths!" the young Disciple exclaimed. "He's going to prove his worth."

Lian noticed how the woman had curled her hands into fists so tight that her knuckles had turned white. She was listening to every word her fellow Disciple was saying with absolute focus, probably making sure he didn't reveal anything important.

"Why would he care about what others thought of his worth?" Lian asked.

"They say he's trying to make an alliance," the young Disciple blurted.

"Drys!" the woman snapped.

Lian lashed out and smacked her across her face. She grunted at the impact, her dark eyes burning with rage.

The male Disciple stared at her. "It's true, then?" he said. Something sparkled in his eyes. He looked so young. He was so inexperienced.

The woman glared at the youngster beside her, knowing that, even in his questions, he was giving away valuable information.

"He really is?" the Disciple asked her. She continued to glare at him without saying a word. The young man then turned to face Lian and Matu again and he grinned a triumphant grin. "He's going to South

America to make an alliance with—"

"Shut up!" the woman shouted, cutting him off. But the Asters had heard enough. They knew everything they needed to know. They knew where Sophie and Sky were, and they knew what Mitrik's plans were. They didn't need these Disciples any longer.

Lian looked over his shoulder at Matu who nodded at him. Lian turned back and took Sky's dagger. They couldn't leave these Disciples alive. Even if they were locked in this room, there was no way of knowing how soon they'd be found. And the Asters didn't need another alarm raised to alert the Underworld to their location. Again.

Lian worked quickly. He gave no warning as he cut the woman's throat. As her blood ran over his hands, he turned to the other Disciple next to her. There was one question they still needed an answer to. Mitrik wouldn't want to transport Sky and Sophie to South America, if he could help it. He'd want the King to come here, the better to show off his prized prisoners and the fighting forces he was amassing.

"Has Mitrik left already?" he asked.

The Disciple looked from Lian to the dead woman. He looked back to Lian and glared at him, knowing now he had said too much. Still, there was this slight hesitation, this slight worry, that told Lian enough. The King wasn't here to protect them. He had already left. Mitrik wasn't wasting any time at all.

Lian turned around and beckoned Matu to come forward. Lian didn't want to use the knife on this Disciple; he didn't want blood staining the man's clothes the way it had done with the woman. If the Asters wanted to get to Mitrik's castle unnoticed, they needed Disciple armour.

Matu stepped forward. The fear was only visible in the Disciple's eyes for a second. A moment later, Matu had placed his hands on either side of the Disciple's face, and snapped his neck. Quick and easy.

When the Disciple was dead, the vines that bound him to the chair unwrapped and vanished back into the ground. Lian looked over his shoulder and found that Nathan was already busy undressing the two male Disciples by the door. Lian doubted either one of them had even regained consciousness before Nathan had his vines tightened around their necks to strangle them.

Fifteen minutes later, the three Asters were dressed in Disciple leathers and armour, making sure the sleeves of their tops covered their Bands. Luckily, most of the clothes fit. Only the jacket Matu was wearing was a little too tight around his large arms and shoulders.

The Asters discarded their own weapons and armed themselves with the weapons of the Disciples. Only one of the three male Disciples had been highly ranked like the woman had been. There were only enough white weapons for two of them. After a short, but lively debate, they decided that Matu would be the single lower ranked Disciple amongst them. It led to a few jokes, which lightened the mood slightly. Lian had his hand on a bone white sword at his hip. The hilt of it felt foreign to his skin.

While they were changing, they briefly spoke about Mitrik's plan. The Disciple had been cut off before mentioning the King's name, but the Asters knew there was no one else in South America worth Mitrik's alliance than the King who killed their future Queen.

But they couldn't think about what a disaster that could become. If they could find Sky and Sophie, then Mitrik would lose his bargaining chip and have no way of proving his worth. So, that was what they had to focus on now.

"I still know the general direction Sophie and Sky were going when I was tracking Sky," Lian said.

Matu nodded. "Good. We'll start with that. When we're deeper in the Underworld we'll find a Disciple along the way to guide us. If that fails, we still have some of Sky's blood, if that tracking still works. If only vaguely."

Matu sheathed the final black dagger into a scabbard strapped around his thigh. "Mitrik is gone; we only have to deal with his inner circle, and we've just eliminated two of those. Sophie and Sky will be working on a way out themselves. We find the white castle, go in, find Sophie and Sky, and destroy the castle from the inside. The inner circle and other Disciples will fight back, but without a King to lead them, they'll be less coordinated. We have a chance to scatter them before the King comes back."

Lian and Nathan nodded. Said like that, the plan seemed so simple, though both of them knew that, chances were, it wouldn't be.

"Sky felt very far away when I was tracking him yesterday. It could take us hours," Lian said.

"We can't run," Nathan pointed out. "That will attract too much attention."

Matu looked at his watch. "We move at normal speed. We go until late tonight and then start again early tomorrow morning. It won't help Sky and Sophie if we're too tired to fight our way back out again."

"You think Sophie and Sky have until tomorrow?" Lian asked, voicing what all three of them feared.

"We know Mitrik just left for South America. It will take a while for him to find the King, win his trust, and convince him to come here. That should take more than a few days," Matu replied. "We stick to this plan. It's our best chance."

Lian nodded.

"All right. Let's go," Matu said. He opened the door and the three of them, dressed as Disciples, headed down the corridor and towards the white castle.

Chapter 9

"Can you open it?" Sophie asked.

Sky was working on the small viewing hatch in the prison door. It could be opened and closed from the outside, but, not surprisingly, there was no obvious way to do so from the inside.

Sky and Sophie had now spent an entire night and day in the prison cell that was kitted out more like a hotel suite. That afternoon, according to Sky's watch, at exactly twelve o'clock, a single Disciple guard had come in and passed a large plateful of roast beef and steamed potatoes through the viewing hatch. It was wide enough to fit a large plate, piled with food, through it.

The latch had shut and was locked the second that Sky had accepted the plate of food. He and Sophie had stared at it, nonplussed.

"I need cutlery, too!" Sky had called, but the Disciple hadn't come back with knives and forks.

The plate still lay untouched at the foot of the four-poster bed. Neither Sky nor Sophie put it past Mitrik to poison the incredibly good-looking plate of food. Though they also thought about the possibility that Mitrik wanted his prisoners to look great for his show for the South American King. What fun would it be if Sky and Sophie came before him all starved, with grey skin and tangled hair? So, there was a slight possibility that Mitrik truly had given them a fantastic plate of food. But they didn't risk it, though the amazing smell was a form of torture in itself. It was another one of Mitrik's jokes.

That day, Sky and Sophie had spent their time coming up with an escape plan. They knew that if they were fast enough, they wouldn't have to deal with Mitrik head-on. Though, killing him would certainly put a stop to the uprising going on outside on the Canyon floor. But for now, the plan was merely to get out of this prison cell.

Sophie and Sky had examined the door in more detail. It weighed a ton, being built from a combination of iron and wood. But it hadn't taken long for them to realise that the door itself wasn't magic proof, which meant that there had to be something else that stopped them from shimmering out.

So, there was some sort of veil that kept them in. The question was, did it match the prison's size exactly? Or did they have some leeway outside of the door?

They turned their attention to the viewing hatch in the door. Sky grunted as he tried to pry it open, but it wouldn't budge. "Dammit," he muttered. He stepped back from the door. He had never been jealous of anyone else's magic, but it would sure have come in handy to be able to break down this door as if it were nothing.

"It's locked on something," Sky said.

"Well, you tried it the nice way," Sophie said. Sky turned around and found that she was standing by one of the lounge chairs at the foot of the four-poster bed. "Let's try it the messy way. Help me break this."

Sky grinned at his sister's ingenuity and walked over. The two of them lifted the lounge chair up off the ground.

"Ready? One, two, three," Sophie counted. And on three they used all their might to throw the chair down on to the ground. The chair broke just like they had hoped. One of the legs took the full weight of the chair and snapped right off. Sky picked it up and headed back for the door. He reached back and threw all his might into bashing the chair leg against the wooden hatch, where Sky thought the lock was sited. Already with the first hit it creaked. With the second hit the hatch splintered at the point of impact, and by the third hit, the hatch swung open.

Sky dropped the chair leg and looked through the hatch. It was about eight by twelve inches in size, which was enough for Sky to poke his head through and see either end of the dungeon corridor. He could see the iron door leading back to the main entrance to his left, and to the end of the corridor to his right. There was no one to be seen.

"What do you see?" Sophie asked.

"Nothing we haven't seen already," Sky said, scanning the space beyond their prison door. "Except... You've got to be kidding me."

"What? What is it?"

The doorway leading back to the main entrance stuck out slightly from the wall, and on the top right corner hung a metal ring. And on that metal ring, a key. Sky could bet anything that it was a key to their prison door. He knew Kali had used the same key for the main entrance as she had for their prison door, so he was almost one hundred per cent sure that this one key could open every single door in this corridor.

"I can see a key," Sky told Sophie.

"*What?*"

"He really does like his games, doesn't he?" Sky muttered. "Dangling our escape just out of our reach."

"You're sure it's out of our reach, right?" Sophie asked. "You can't shimmer it to you?"

"No. I've already tried shimmering outside of this cell into the hallway. If I can't get there from here, then I can't get something from there to here either. The stupid veil is in the way."

"Where does it start?"

Sky pulled his head back into the room and turned to look at her. "What?"

"Where does the veil start?" Sophie's eyes were clear and bright; the way they always were when she'd thought of something.

"You know sometimes when you think you're explaining something, you're really not," Sky said.

Sophie rolled her eyes and batted her brother away from the door so that she could look through the hatch. "If this veil is like the one around the Grand Canyon, then it's a physical thing. We couldn't get through the one outside; it was like walking against an invisible barrier. But the human hikers could pass through, no problem."

"But we didn't pass through anything physical coming in here. And he couldn't have put it up without even being here," Sky pointed out.

"Which means the bonds around our wrists, which were his magic, too, got us through this veil without us even noticing," Sophie thought aloud. She pushed Sky out of the way and stood up on her toes so that her shoulders were level with the hatch. She put her arm through it. She had barely stretched her arm fifteen inches outside when her hand flattened against something invisible. Sophie turned to look at Sky, her thunderstorm grey eyes sparkling. "Don't you see what this means?"

Sky stared at Sophie, then at her flat hand against the physical veil just fifteen inches outside of their prison door, and then back at Sophie again. He didn't know what it meant. Fifteen inches wasn't a wide enough space for him to shimmer to, even if Sophie now proved it was possible. That veil would probably reach all along the walls across each prison door, and it would definitely stop at the main entrance. Which meant that even if he could fit into the fifteen inches, *which he couldn't*, he still wouldn't get close enough to the key to get them out.

"Not everyone has magic to make themselves a genius like you." Though Sky did notice that Sophie's Band wasn't even glowing.

"It means that we needed bonds to get us through, but Kali walked through with nothing, remember? Mitrik's Second, too. They didn't need anything, just like the human hikers didn't need anything to get through Mitrik's veil," Sophie explained.

Sky raised his eyebrows. "So?"

"*So...* What is the one thing that makes us different from humans, and from Disciples and from Kings and from Affinites? What is the one thing that makes us all different?"

"Our magic, specifically. But otherwise... our blood," Sky realised. "But even so, we're still trapped here because of it. Does this realisation mean anything useful?"

Sophie pulled back her arm and turned to the dungeon, her eyes scanning the room. The Band on her wrist had now started to glow as her eyes glided over every piece of furniture. "It means I know how we're going to get out of here."

The following afternoon Sky stared at his watch and sighed. It could take another five minutes, or it could take another hour, for a Disciple to come in and bring them whatever beautiful plate of food Mitrik's chefs would serve them today.

It was two minutes to twelve o'clock.

Yesterday the Disciple had come bang on twelve. Was that just a coincidence?

Sky was leaning against the door, with his head tilted to the hatch so that he still had a view of the main entrance to the prison cells. He needed to be ready the second a Disciple would step through that veil to bring them their food. He glanced at Sophie. She was kneeling by the trapdoor, busy unscrewing the iron ring that was needed to pull the trapdoor open. Sky wondered if the other end of what that ring was attached to would be sharp enough for their plan to work.

Sophie had explained her plan to him, and Sky had to admit that what she had come up with was absolutely insane – insanely ingenious. Not in a million years would he have come up with it himself. But the way that Sophie explained the logic... and the physics; her plan might be insane, but it might just work. And it might also be their only way out of here.

"Yeah, this should do it," Sophie said. Sky looked at his sister again to see what she had found; attached to the end of the ring to pull the trapdoor open, was a long thick screw. The end of it seemed pointy and sharp enough to inflict some serious damage. Sadly, Mitrik hadn't been cocky enough to leave them their weapons.

The King had been cocky enough to leave that key there, though. Sky wondered why the King was so keen on continuing these games even when he wasn't around to step in if one of them didn't work out the way he planned. Was he really that full of himself? Sky had a really hard time placing the King—he had these moments when he almost seemed human. Then he acted like an idiot, but he wasn't stupid. Far from it.

But the King was still an idiot.

Sky's magic hummed through his veins. He could feel that laser focus descend upon him. He didn't feel his hunger. The feeling of fear about Lian's safety was muted. This was their one chance to break out of here. No other chance had come before this. It was best to focus on getting this one right.

Only having one shot should scare him; should make him cautious or nervous. But it didn't. It excited him. This was what he was good at. Sky wasn't the one with the brilliant plans like Sophie, or like Nathan occasionally. And he didn't have the calm, rational energy of Matu, who could then also become utterly ruthless. No. He was the unexpected force to be reckoned with. He was that split second between control and impulse, between the calm and the storm. Between life and death.

And that's what made him so dangerous.

Sky pinned back his ears. In the distance he could hear footsteps descending the stairs on the other side of the iron door leading to the prison cells.

Twelve o'clock.

Bang on time.

"Someone's coming," he said quietly.

Sophie walked over and took her place a few feet away from the hatch, so she would be right in view for the person on the other side.

"What if they know exactly where the veil starts?" Sky asked her. He'd asked the question before. He needed to know that Sophie was sure of her answer.

"They'll still need to pass through it to give us that food. Maybe just a hand, but it will be enough," Sophie said. She'd said those exact words before. She didn't mock him or make fun of him for asking again. This was their only chance. They both knew the importance of getting it right in one go.

A key turned in a lock, and the iron door swung open. Without putting his head through the hatch, Sky peered through the gap and saw two Disciples enter the prison corridor. Neither Disciple was the one who had given them their food the day before. Sky looked over at Sophie and raised two fingers in the air. Sophie nodded at his gesture and turned her attention back to the door. They had hoped for one. Just the one Disciple would've been easiest. But they could manage two. If they were fast enough.

Neither Disciple was wearing any armour. They did each have a weapons belt around their waist. Sky immediately noted that neither Disciple had bone white weapons in their sheathes. But there was no way of knowing what their affinities were. Sky could only hope that it had nothing to do with sensing danger or any form of attack.

Both Disciples were male. One had a long brown pony tail, while the other had a shaven head. The man with the shaven head looked to be in his thirties or forties, while the other was about Sky's age. The younger one seemed to be the more nervous of the two. Sky wondered how long he had worked in Mitrik's dungeons.

The bald Disciple closed the iron door behind them. The younger Disciple was holding a tray of food; it looked like spare ribs with mashed potatoes and a thick, glossy sauce. It smelt delicious, and Sky's empty stomach growled in reaction. If there hadn't been the possibility of the food containing poison, Sky would've gladly finished the entire plate by himself.

The younger Disciple handed the tray of food to his superior and then remained by the door. Sky watched as the older Disciple walked over to their prison cell. Sky remained to the side of the door where the Disciple couldn't see him. The bald Disciple looked straight at the hatch, and Sky could detect his surprise when he found it broken open and Sophie staring right back at him.

One tiny nod of her head would be enough of a signal, but it never came. Sky turned his head towards the hatch, but from this angle he couldn't see the Disciple.

"Where is the other one?" the Disciple growled suspiciously.

He wasn't a complete idiot, Sky thought. Such a shame.

It didn't matter. Plan B would work just as well.

Sky moved from his spot and stepped in front of the hatch. He stared at the bald Disciple. He was standing right behind the veil. Sky looked past him and saw that it was the younger Disciple who was holding the keys to the main entrance, and probably also to their cell.

Sky cursed internally, but kept his face neutral.

"Step back," the bald Disciple barked.

Sky threw the man a grin. "Afraid of me?"

The Disciple snarled. "I don't take chances."

"Oh, you should," Sky said lightly as he took a swaggering step back. "Gambling could earn you big bucks, my friend. More than you could ever earn here, that's for sure."

"Quit your rambling," the man snapped.

Sky chuckled.

"Hold out your hand," the Disciple commanded.

Sky held out his left hand.

"The other one," the Disciple growled.

"All right, all right. Calm down," Sky said nonchalantly. He held out his right hand, the Band on his wrist fully exposed. The swirling lines were black. He wasn't using any magic, which was exactly what the Disciple wanted to see. The Disciple stared at the Band on Sky's wrist for a long moment, before finally deciding that it was safe for him to offer the food. He was holding the tray in his left hand, and slowly brought it towards the hatch.

Sky made sure he maintained his nonchalant stance as the tip of the tray now passed through the veil. Sky had spent the last hour testing and feeling the veil so that he knew exactly where it was without having to touch it.

The Disciple shuffled forward, but kept his body firmly on the other side of the veil. He knew exactly where the veil started, too, but with the distance between him and the hatch, the Disciple would have to pass at least his hand through the veil to get the tray within Sky's reach.

Sky held his right hand steady, making sure that he was still harness-ing no magic at all and the lines of his Band remained black. From what the Disciple could see, his upper body was still relaxed, but from the waist down, his feet and legs were strained with tension, and ready to pounce once the Disciple's hand breached the veil.

Sky leaned slowly forward with his hand to reach for the tray of food. The Disciple was tracking his every move. Sky chuckled lightly at the Disciple's focus. His light and airy manner seemed to have the desired effect. Even though the Disciple was being extremely careful, he wasn't expecting anything.

Not until it was too late.

Sky waited for the tray to come close to his fingers. He could tell that the tips of the Disciple's fingers had passed through the veil. The Disciple reached in further, so that Sky could take the tray from him. But in doing so, his entire hand was now on their side of the veil.

It happened in a flash.

Sky's Band glowed.

He shot forward with a speed faster than humanly possible. He snatched the Disciple's hand before he'd had the time to retract it to the safe side of the veil. Sky dug his nails in the Disciple's skin and then shot back from the door, pulling the arm of the Disciple straight through the hatch. At that speed the Disciple had no way of protecting himself as he crashed against the other side of the door. The side of his head hit the door with a sickening crunch. Sky pulled the Disciple's arm to the left. The man screamed as bones cracked in his shoulder.

As fast as lightning, Sky let go of the Disciple's hand; then reached through the hatch and locked both of his hands around the Disciple's throat. He used his speed again to pull backwards to bash the Disciple's head back against the edge of the hatch a few times.

It all happened in a matter of seconds.

Sophie was by his side, screw in hand. The man was clawing at Sky's hands, but Sky dug his nails in the Disciple's throat and made sure that he didn't let go. Sky could strangle the man right there, but they needed his blood to flow.

Sophie reached over Sky's arms, through the hatch, and around the Disciple's neck. She stabbed the end of the screw right above Sky's hands into the Disciple's throat, at the back of his jaw, just underneath the ear. She tore a gash through his skin.

Blood sprayed, coating Sky's hands as he held on to the thrashing Disciple as Sophie cut and sawed through the Disciple's skin. It was messy and it didn't work as well as it would've done with a knife, but the blood flowed freely enough.

The blood covered Sky's hands. It was sticky and warm and absolutely disgusting. The man had already stopped clawing at Sky's hands. The strength was leaving his body as the life drained out of him.

Sky kept a hold of the man for as long as he could, making sure as much blood as possible coated his hands before letting him go. Sky then tried to angle the Disciple's fall in such a way that he wouldn't be lying with his dead weight against the door. It just about worked; half his body lay in front of the door, while the other half was more to the side.

Panting, Sky looked from his sticky, red hands towards the iron door. It was closed still, but the younger Disciple was nowhere to be seen. Sky assumed that he had fled in panic, locking the iron door behind him. And in his panic to get out, he hadn't thought to take the second key with him.

"The other one is gone," Sky said.

"That doesn't matter right now." Sophie was looking at his hands. "It looked like you caught plenty."

Sky looked down. His hands were completely covered in the Disciple's blood. An immature part of him wanted to flick some of the blood in Sophie's face. But instead, he turned around and started on the last part of her plan. If this didn't work, it wouldn't make any difference that the second key was still there.

Sky stuck his blood-soaked hand through the hatch and reached forward. He waited for that invisible physical barrier to block him, but it didn't happen. He had touched it plenty of times in the hours before the Disciples had come to know that his hand was now past it.

"It worked," Sky said unbelievably. He heard Sophie release a breath of relief behind him. He smiled to himself. His sister really was a genius. Sky turned to look at the key hooked to the top right corner of the main entrance. He focused on his magic and felt his Band pulse on his blood splattered wrist.

There was a small flash of blue light and the key vanished. A second later there was another blue flash, this time around Sky's hand, and he felt the metal key land in his hand. He clasped his fingers around it immediately, and retracted his hand from outside the veil and back through the hatch.

He turned towards Sophie and opened up his hand, revealing the key. Sophie stared at it, and then looked up and smiled brilliantly at him.

Sky smiled back and turned to their prison door. He slid the key in the lock and prayed that this wasn't one of Mitrik's jokes again.

The key fit in the lock, and Sky turned it. There was no resistance as he turned the key for a whole circle.

There was a click, and the door opened a few inches into the room.

Sky pulled on the door and looked stupidly at the hallway beyond. All that effort in making sure the Disciple didn't fall right in front of the door so they wouldn't be able to open it... "I forgot the door opens this way, not out."

Sophie chuckled and came to stand next to him to pat him on the shoulder. "Yeah, well. You pride yourself on being the best, but you're still an idiot."

Sky huffed. "I still did pretty good."

Sophie smiled up at her brother. "Yeah, you did pretty *well*."

Sky narrowed his eyes. "Don't judge me with your fancy English speaking."

"It's not just the English, you dumb Aussie."

They both laughed.

Sky was about to step over the Disciple and out of the cell, when Sophie said, "Wait!"

He turned to look at her. "What?"

She was staring at him with a disgusted look on her face. "As much as I hate the idea of it, I'm going to have to hold your hand to get out of here."

"Why?"

"Because the door wasn't what kept us out, remember? It's the veil, and without that Disciple blood I can't get through."

Sky grinned as he offered Sophie his bloodied hand. Sophie groaned softly before taking it in hers. They stepped over the dead Disciple and through the veil without a problem.

Sky looked back at the cell and said, "Come on. It won't be long until the alarm is raised—"

A sudden wave of nausea hit him. A whole array of sounds crashed into his head. Sky clutched his head as the sounds became words; became screams. He heard Lian call his name over and over again in his head. And then came Matu's voice, calling his name as well. And then Lian again. And then Matu again. Lian's voice sounded weaker with every time he called Sky's name. But it wasn't just his name. It was more.

Sky!

Sky!

Sky, I need you!

Sky, I need you now!

Then Matu's voice.

Sky! Lian needs you!

Sky!

Then Lian's again.

Sky, Matu and Nathan can't help me...

Sky, I need Sophie...

Suddenly, through all the shouting and calling, Sky knew it was the veil around the prison that had stopped him from hearing the calls. And he was now hearing them all at once. His head felt like it was about to explode. And the sound of Lian's voice was awful. It kept getting weaker and weaker. And then suddenly he didn't hear Lian's voice anymore. A void opened up in Sky's head where he hoped Lian would still be calling him. Where he hoped Lian would call his name, just to say he was all right. But there was nothing. And the true weakness of Lian's voice the last time he called Sky's name...

Sky knew enough.

Matu and Nathan couldn't help Lian.

He knew he and Sophie couldn't have got out of the prison earlier than now. But still. But still...

Lian...

His brother, his mirror. The only one of the Asters who didn't take life so seriously, just like him. That light, that loyalty...

"Sky!"

At the sound of her voice, his heart broke.

"No, no, no, no..." he moaned, digging his nails into his skull.

"Sky!" Sophie called again. Her hands were on his, and she was trying to bring them away from his head. Sky stilled at her touch. He let her guide his hands back down to his side. He opened his eyes and looked at her.

"What happened?" she asked. She had a terribly worried look on her face.

Sky stared at her for a moment. He took a few seconds to answer. A few seconds longer for her to be pleased that her plan had got them out of the prison cell. A few seconds for her to still believe he was alive.

After taking a deep breath he said, "Lian's dead."

It was like she froze for a moment. Then her eyes widened. "What happened? How do you know?"

Sky gestured to the prison door with his head. "I couldn't hear their calls when we were inside the veil. I just got them all at once. Lian kept calling me. Saying he couldn't get to Matu and Nathan. Even Matu called and said we needed to find Lian. And his voice, Soph... He kept calling... It kept getting weaker and weaker, until..."

He bit his bottom lip.

Sophie closed her eyes. A moment later she had her arms wrapped

97

around him.

"I'm so sorry you had to hear that," Sophie whispered.

Sky gritted his teeth, praying that she'd stop there. He couldn't bear to hear her say those words again. The words he'd heard so often ever since Gayle had died.

There was nothing you could have done.

But there always was. He could've stopped sooner to heal Sophie's leg. They wouldn't have ended up on the marble path that led to the white castle. They wouldn't have been taken captive. He would've heard Lian's call.

Lian would still be alive.

He would still be...

Sophie gave one squeeze and let go of him. Sky looked at her face as she stepped back and looked up at him. There were no tears. There was no sadness. There was only anger. Her grey eyes were a true storm now.

"Let's make them pay for it," she snarled. The rage in her gave him energy. It gave him what he needed to turn this void that had suddenly opened up, into something horribly threatening and dangerous.

Somewhere distant in the castle an alarm went off, signalling their escape. Neither of them paid any attention to it.

"You have an idea?"

"We destroy them from the inside out." Sophie turned away from him and headed for the iron door. "Starting with taking down this whole bloody building."

Chapter 10

The Amazon Rainforest was hot and humid and horrible. Even with Rose using her magic of Flora to clear a wide enough path, Madeleine felt claustrophobic and sticky.

The three Ceders had been in the Amazon for two days now. Diallo's death hadn't settled yet within Madeleine. She could still see him, every time she blinked; every time her mind drifted for even a second. Over and over again she saw that blade being pulled across his throat. It made her feel sick every time.

After she and Rose helped Katherine wrap Diallo's body in a clean sheet, Madeleine sent Diallo's body back to Saluverus' morgue. Madeleine couldn't stop thinking about what the pathologists might find. Guilty as it made her feel, Madeleine hoped they found something. She wanted a good reason. A reason why he couldn't call her sooner; why he couldn't call for help. Why he didn't fight back. Why he died.

Madeleine balled her fists and tried to focus. But she was distracted. She couldn't help it. She'd lost three of her fellow Ceders in a matter of weeks. All in the same place; all because of the same man. And here they were, making their way through the Amazon jungle, instead of storming the Underworld like her body and magic ached for her to do.

The killed Affinites were sent back together with Diallo's body. They had all been identified. That morning, the Small Council had informed them of the identity of the two Affinites still missing: Ecuadorian archaeologist Rosanna Zambrano and biologist Myat Kyu from Myanmar.

Madeleine didn't know either of them. They had come to the Amazon with Diallo because of their respective specialities. They weren't soldiers. How these two were the ones possibly still alive was beyond Madeleine. Though her belief that they were in fact still alive was hanging by a thread. These two Affinites were incredibly smart. They could have calculated that the only chance they had of surviving was to run and hide while the others were attacked.

That made them cowards. But alive, perhaps.

And they must have gone into hiding. Only Rose, with her connection to the nature around them, had any chance at finding them if Disciples hadn't done so already.

Rose led the way through the dense vegetation. Her Band was glowing green on her wrist as she made a path in front of her and stayed in contact with the nature around her at the same time. Even so, progress was slow.

The trees sensed many things. They could've sensed the Affinites run past them. They would be able to give Rose a sense of direction as to where they had gone or where they had been taken.

Still, none of it told Madeleine how the Affinites had managed to run off without her seeing them. She'd left the sleeping tent so quickly after Diallo's death. The ambush couldn't have begun long before that. They couldn't have got far.

And yet, for some reason, the three Ceders were roaming further and further away from the camp, with no sign of the Affinites or their escape route.

Madeleine knew they weren't just in the Amazon to find the biologist and archaeologist. The Ambassador had called them the evening before. There was still a part of Axel Reed that wanted to know what had happened. So many Affinites were dead. Percy Kelly still hadn't improved. He was the only Affinite alive who could tell them what had happened; what had attacked him. They needed to know.

Madeleine wasn't worried about her own safety. She, Rose and Katherine were on high alert. As long as they stayed together, Madeleine was confident all three of them would make it out of Brazil alive if whatever had attacked everyone else, attacked them. Especially with her shimmer. Madeleine just hoped she'd keep a clear enough head to shimmer out, instead of falling into a blind rage at what had happened to Diallo. If she and these powerful women in front of her came face to face with the King, or anyone else high up in his ranks, Madeleine didn't know what would happen. If it looked like they would lose the fight, would she use her shimmer? Walking away then would be the hardest thing to do.

"Anything?" Madeleine called out to Rose.

"Close..." Rose murmured softly.

Madeleine's head shot up. She'd been following Rose and Katherine for hours now, keeping her eyes on the jungle to the left of her. Katherine had been doing the same on the right. This was the first time Rose sounded as if she had sensed something.

Rose slowed in front of them until she eventually stopped. Madeleine looked past Katherine towards her. Rose's Band was glowing strong and steady as she studied the greenery around her. Madeleine couldn't imagine what she was doing; if she was actually having a conversation with the trees as though they had voices. Madeleine knew it was more complicated than that. Vaguer. More sensations, feelings.

Rose looked back over her shoulder and past the two Ceders standing behind her. Her eyes were unfocused. She wasn't seeing what was in front of her; she was lost deep within her magic. She turned her head and took a single step forward. She looked around herself again, as if this single step made all the difference.

"We need to be heading in that direction," Rose said, and pointed.

Madeleine followed Rose's finger. She frowned and pulled a compass out of her pocket.

"But that's in the opposite direction to the nearest entrance to the South American Underworld," Madeleine pointed out. If the archaeologist and biologist were still alive, as the Ceders hoped they were, they'd expected the Affinites to be taken towards the entrance, and underground. The fact that they were not heading towards the entrance suggested what Madeleine had already feared: that the Ceders were too late and the Affinites had already been killed and dumped back on the Surface. Of course, there was also the possibility that they were still alive and in hiding. Though from everything that had happened in the Amazon Rainforest in the past weeks, Madeleine doubted that would be the case.

Rose gave both her and Katherine a sad look. "I don't know what to tell you. It's what I'm sensing."

Katherine put a hand on her shoulder. "It's all right. You have to follow that sense. It's all we have to go on."

Madeleine kept her mouth shut, and Rose led them away from the entrance to the Underworld.

The three of them hiked through the Amazon for another two hours. They didn't say much along the way. Rose just kept her focus on the lead she seemed to have found, while Katherine and Madeleine constantly scanned their surroundings for potential ambushes. Madeleine had her hand on the Disciple's dagger at her waist at all times. She tried not to think about how it was the dagger that was used to kill Diallo. Though that thought made her tighten her grip on it more.

Another hour passed. At a certain point Madeleine could hear the sound of running water in the distance.

"Are we close to a river?" Katherine asked, hearing it, too.

"Not one of the main ones," Rose replied.

As they continued, the sound of rushing water increased. When the river came into view, it wasn't as wide as she'd expected it to be, but it was still one the Ceders couldn't cross easily. The water rushed past at quite some speed. Foam and miniature whirlpools broke the surface where rocks lay just underneath the surface.

Madeleine immediately scanned the rapids, but realised her shimmer could get them to the other side a lot easier and dryer. She was about to offer it as an option to the others, when she saw what Rose was doing.

The Ceder of Flora was kneeling by the river. She reached out her right hand and stuck it in the water. For a moment she moved her hand back and forth, before pulling it out again.

"This river joins up with one of the larger ones that leads to the ocean," she said.

Madeleine waited for Rose to continue, but she didn't. "So?" Madeleine pushed. She knew she needed to be careful. Where Madeleine's reaction to Diallo's death had been rage, Rose had been overwhelmed and devastated. Everything she did was with an ounce of extra hesitation. Everything she did was slightly slower, as if she was watching life go by in fast forward, and Rose was still going the regular speed.

Her behaviour had been worrying at first, as the Ceders had started their search a day ago. But when, a few hours ago, at one suspicious sound, Rose had snapped back to focus so quickly, Madeleine forgot why she'd ever been worried. It was just in the quiet moments, when there was too much time to think and remember, that Rose's beaten demeanour returned.

"I think a body was disposed of in the river," Rose said absently. "We need to hurry if we want to catch it before it's swept out to sea."

Abruptly, she started walking along the riverbed. A low branch blocked her path, but with nothing more than a simple wave of her hand, the tree morphed and the branch moved out of her way.

Katherine gave Madeleine a nervous glance before following Rose along the river. Madeleine felt slightly dumbfounded by Rose's com-

103

ment, and blankly followed the Ceder of Health and Knowledge.

As fast as Rose had started downstream, she'd stopped. Madeleine couldn't see anything as Katherine was blocking her view.

"What's going on?" Madeleine asked.

"We didn't need to hurry after all," Rose said softly.

Neither Katherine, nor Rose, got out of the way for Madeleine to see what had happened. Her patience ran out, and, frustrated, Madeleine dug into her magic. She flew around Katherine and Rose so that she was hovering right above the river. She descended closer to Rose to see what she'd found.

Bile rose in her throat when she saw.

There was no mistaking the Affinite clothing. Even though Madeleine had never met the Affinites they were looking for, she knew this could be none other than Myat Kya, the biologist from Myanmar. Though not all of him was here. His right arm, all the way up to and including his shoulder were missing; ripped off, it seemed. And up until his thigh, the rest of his left leg was missing, as well.

Madeleine glanced at the other two women for a moment. Katherine had her hands clapped over her mouth, and Rose was sniffling slightly. A tear was rolling down her cheek. Usually, all three of them were stone-cold and could be clinical and focused in these situations. Madeleine had done her work perfectly when she and Sky shimmered to Brazil after he'd saved Percy. But she couldn't hold in her disgust now; her revulsion. Her anger bubbled close to the surface. It took all her effort not to grab the nearest rock or branch and throw it across the river.

The horror of what this new King was capable of. The atrocity of his crimes; of how he treated the Affinites he captured. Madeleine had seen nothing like it. She had never seen limbs ripped off of bodies. She could practically still see the scream on Myat's face.

Madeleine closed her eyes and swallowed. Still hovering, she reached into her pocket and pulled out her phone. She dialled Axel's number and waited for the Ambassador to pick up.

"Madeleine. What did you find?"

Madeleine looked down at Myat Kya's body and said simply, "We found a body."

It was the one meeting Axel had been dreading all day. By himself, he headed down the basement steps of the castle. At the second-to-bottom floor, Axel pushed through the door that said *Authorised personnel only.* On the other side of the door he walked down the stairs to the basement. Only the morgue, pathology labs and static portals were down here. Aside from the doctors, only the Small Council and the Asters had access.

Sylvia had offered to come with him, but Axel wanted to go alone.

Of all the new bodies the morgue had received from South America, Axel had wanted the pathologists to start on Diallo's first. He'd heard from a terribly angry Madeleine that Diallo's eyes were droopy when the Disciple held him up, and that he didn't even fight back. *Find out why*, were her words shouted down the phone.

Axel couldn't believe it himself. How the Ceder of Strength had been killed so easily; there had to be more to it.

There was only one man in the pathology labs when he entered. Doctor Akande stood with his back towards the Ambassador. When the door closed, he turned around.

"Ambassador," Doctor Akande said in acknowledgment. At first sight, he seemed calm, with his shoulders relaxed arms hanging loosely at his sides. But he wasn't; right after he acknowledged Axel, Doctor Akande cast his eyes down, avoiding eye contact with the Ambassador.

Axel nodded his head. "Taye."

Axel looked around the room. He'd expected to see Diallo's body on one of the tables in the room, but they were all empty. The room was bare and clean. No surgical tools were anywhere to be seen; all carefully put away.

"Tell me you found something," Axel said.

The small, Nigerian doctor placed his hands on the table in front of him. The look on his face told Axel enough. He'd found something. Axel just couldn't tell if it was bad, or if it was terrible.

"I found traces of poison in his blood," Doctor Akande said.

Axel suddenly felt lost for words. Eventually he ground out, "Poison?"

"Yes. Snake poison."

"The camp was poisoned before it was attacked?"

Taye Akande shook his head. "Not the camp. Just Mr. Madaki."

Axel stared at the pathologist.

"And it looks like it wasn't a strategic manoeuvre on the King's side," Doctor Akande continued.

Axel frowned. "What do you mean?"

"Come and look at this," Taye said. The pathologist turned around and opened a drawer. Axel stepped closer and stood on the other side of the table. When Taye faced Axel once again he was holding a brown folder. He opened it and placed one large photograph on the table. From where Axel stood, the whole picture was a uniform dark brown.

"What am I looking at?" Axel asked.

"It's a picture of Mr. Madaki's skin, zoomed in considerably. See here—" Axel leaned in to where Taye Akande pointed at two darker spots now visible even against Diallo's dark skin, "—These are bite marks."

"Bite marks?"

Doctor Akande straightened. "Uh-hum. The attack was planned. We can tell that by the other bodies, and our determinations of the place and times of death. But they wouldn't have succeeded if a snake bite hadn't paralysed Mr. Madaki right before."

"You've got to be joking," was all that Axel could say.

Doctor Akande cast his eyes down. "I'm afraid not."

Axel slammed his hands on the table. "*How is that possible?*"

The pathologist flinched and took an instinctive step backwards. He was a scrawny little man. Even when calm, the Ambassador was intimidating to him.

Doctor Akande waited anxiously for Axel's next move. The Ambassador had asked a question, but Taye assumed it was rhetorical.

Axel held up his hands. "I apologise," he said. "I just... You're telling me, that the Ceder of Strength got bitten by a snake the same night as a planned Disciple attack?"

Doctor Akande looked warily at the Ambassador. "Yes," he said softly.

"And that his paralysis is why the entire camp is in the morgue right now?"

"Knowing what we know about the Ceder of Strength and his magic—"

"Doctor..." Axel growled.

"Yes," Doctor Akande squeaked. "Yes, he was paralysed, which prevented him from fighting; from moving."

"Wouldn't he have felt the bite?"

The pathologist shook his head. "Not necessarily, no. Not if he was in his REM sleep. It could have felt no different to a mosquito bite. I'm afraid bites like these happen more often than you think."

"And the poison would work that fast?" Axel said.

Doctor Akande placed the picture back in the brown folder and put it back in the drawer behind him. "There are poisons that work that fast, yes," he said. Being asked questions based on the science and his work seemed to have put him back at ease. "I could do further testing to see which poison it was and determine when in the night he was bitten and how quickly the paralysis took hold—"

"No," Axel interrupted.

"Ambassador?"

Axel shook his head. "No more testing. It won't change the outcome. It won't change the fact that a stupid snake bite is the reason another six Affinites are dead in a pathology lab. We know what killed Diallo; it doesn't matter exactly which bloody poison or which bloody snake. Don't waste your time and resources on that. Finish the report and prepare his body for burning. I want this closed off."

Doctor Akande looked at him for a moment. Axel could tell that the order to stop his work was not one he liked. That was why Taye Akande was the leading pathologist on Saluverus. He was more thorough and detailed than anyone who had ever worked there. But this time Axel didn't want extra detail. He wanted this finished. This horrible, terrible chapter in Aster and Affinite history closed off and locked away.

Eventually, Doctor Akande inclined his head. "As you wish."

"It is what I wish," Axel said. "Thank you for the information"

And with nothing else needing to be said between them, Axel turned around and left the pathology lab. He climbed the stairs, his thoughts boiling in his head. He didn't stop at the ground floor but continued all the way up to the top floor, to the Throne Room. It was completely deserted. Axel walked in between the rows of benches all the way to the alter. To the right of the alter was a small door. He walked through it and found himself in a smaller room.

It was a small chapel. It had several rows of short benches on either side. Front and centre stood a stone statue of Aiyana. In most paintings of her, Aiyana wore battle armour, holding her mythical sword and shield, said to be gifted with the same powers as she had. And she was usually surrounded by ferocious beasts. From lions and tigers to wolves and crocodiles. But not here. In this little place of worship, she wore a long dress. Her hair, instead of being tied in thick braids, hung loosely down her back and shoulders. She was holding out her hands, like a mother would if her child had fallen down and she offered to help them stand back up again. And even in stone, her eyes and smile were so warm, Axel could feel the care and love she had for her people.

Around her feet, in a half circle, were three lines of tea lights. The tiny candles were all burning brightly. They were spelled. They never stopped burning.

Axel looked up at Aiyana's face. He felt completely drained, hollow. He'd failed her.

Her reincarnation had come to this world, almost five hundred years after she had left it. And Axel had failed to keep her safe; to bring her here. And even after that, he'd failed. Everything he'd done after that, was a failure. He couldn't find their bodies. He couldn't give them a proper burial. He couldn't get the Aster magic to live on; the magic that she had created. There would be no new lines of Aster magic beyond the five found in the current generation. And there was no new Queen to help them fight whatever threat Gayle's birth had predicted.

And it had all happened on his watch.

Axel sank down onto a bench in the first row and buried his face in his hands.

The speech therapist and the psychotherapist had wanted to be there when Percy Kelly was moved from the Medical Bay up into the cliffs. There was a small shack, nestled at the base between two cliff peaks, that

Jackson and his brother used to play in when they were little. Neither of them knew who had built it, or who had lived in it. For as long as Jackson could remember, the shack had been empty. But all throughout their youth, once he and Percy had transferred to Saluverus, this had been like a second home to them. Their playhouse. Their base camp. Their secret escape.

The shack was a single square room, with a tiny, battered cooking area, a wonky table with only two chairs, and a bed that had seen better days. There was a small bathroom in the back with just a compost toilet and a makeshift shower. It was small and old, but it was enough. Jackson would make sure some renovations would be done over time, but not now. Now it needed to be something Percy recognised and felt comfortable in.

Jackson hated the idea of Percy being out here; needing to be out of everyone's way so he wouldn't be a danger to anyone. He didn't want to think about what Percy had gone through in the Amazon. Like Jackson, his brother had been trained and equipped to be able to face anything. And in the long years they served Saluverus together, they had faced plenty. So what had the South American King done that had been so shocking and so traumatising that it could break the mind of Saluverus' best Affinite soldier? It was the one question they were all wondering, but were not saying out loud.

Jackson sighed and stared down the path.

"It will be all right," Olga Masalis said. "This is what is best for him right now."

Jackson turned to the psychotherapist. "It's not that... Do you think there is a chance he will get back to who he was?"

"It is hard to say. I've treated many patients with trauma. It is clear your brother suffers from post-traumatic stress. He imagines things that aren't there. He sometimes thinks he's back there, and he blindly panics and attacks. Those are classic symptoms I understand. But his fear of magic is unclear to me still. And the loss of his speech is tied in with it as well—also unusual. Arnar Jakobsson and I will do everything in our power to help your brother. But these things do take time."

Jackson nodded. It wasn't what he wanted to hear, but he knew he wasn't going to get a better response than that.

There was movement down the narrow, rocky path, and a whole line of people appeared. Jackson saw his brother first, sitting in a wheelchair with his leg up in a cast. The nurse, Dagmara, was pushing the wheelchair. One of Percy's best soldiers walked diagonally behind Dagmara; the path only just being wide enough for two people to walk closely side by side. Behind him came Bianka Mazur, Jillian and Arthur. Then a few feet behind them walked Axel Reed and Doctor Arnar Jakobsson.

Jackson tried to meet Jillian's gaze as the party filed out into the open space at the front of the shack, but she kept her eyes on the ground. She looked like a ghost. Her skin was pale and she had great bags under her eyes. Jackson knew she hadn't had a good night sleep since her father came back to the island. The bubbly, warm girl was as different to this grieving, depressed girl as day and night.

Jackson worried terribly about her. He knew Arthur was trying to take care of her, but Jackson knew from his son that Jillian didn't want to see anyone about her sleeping problems or her mental state. In that regard she was just like her parents. Jackson hoped he and Arthur could convince her to change her mind soon.

Jackson turned to the other people present. Bianka and Percy's soldier followed Dagmara as she pushed Percy inside the shack. Jillian, Arthur and Arnar Jakobsson remained in the door opening. Axel stayed outside with Jackson and Olga Masalis.

"How soon will he be able to talk again?" Axel asked harshly.

"There is no way to say," Olga answered.

"I understand that you're doing everything you can to bring him back, but you have to understand that—" Axel glanced at Jillian, Arthur and the speech therapist to be was sure they couldn't hear him, "—that I have three Ceders in the Amazon right now, close to where Diallo and his camp were murdered. And it would be a great help if they knew what they were up against, should they run into trouble."

Jackson glanced at the shack as well. Diallo's death wasn't known anywhere outside of the Small Council and Olga. Axel wanted to keep it that way until the Asters returned from North America. The Ambassador didn't want Matu hearing the news about his father from anybody else than him.

Axel turned to Jackson and offered him a look that told him that the Ambassador was sorry to have to push on this matter. Jackson inclined his head in understanding. He wanted his brother to recover more than anyone, but he knew the information Percy had was even more important. Before he left for Brazil, Percy would've wanted to do anything to help the Small Council. If the speech therapist would have to push the soldier to speak of his experiences, even though that could hinder his mental recovery significantly, Jackson knew his brother would still do it. Percy believed in Saluverus, and the Asters, Ceders and Elders, as much as Jackson did. The twin brothers believed in their purpose and what they stood for. And Percy would've done all he could to help.

"I'm sorry, but I cannot push the protocol. I am working in the best interest of the patient," Olga said, not at all cowed by Axel's comment.

"I'm not interested in sorry," Axel said, his voice the one of a ruthless leader. "You get me the information I need sooner rather than later. You might be working in the best interest of the patient, but if one terminal case is the price for keeping three Ceders alive to protect the world from any of the Kings re-surfacing, then that is a price Soldier Kelly would pay any day."

Jackson glanced at the psychotherapist. He knew he had to say it, but at the same he hated the words that came out of his mouth as he told Olga, "He would."

Olga glanced at Jackson, surprise in her eyes. She opened her mouth to respond to Axel when his phone started to ring. Axel held up his hand and said, "Excuse me," and walked away.

"I need to do what is in the best interest of your brother," Olga repeated. Arnar Jakobsson joined the two of them.

Jackson met Olga's gaze. He thought of his niece. She had already lost her mother. She deserved to have a parent. And yet, with all his honour and integrity towards Saluverus and the Small Council bearing down on him, he said, "Let me be clear. I want my brother back. I want my niece to have a father again. But you are not here for me or for her; you are here on the orders of the Small Council. Even though I am a part of that, my emotions do not weigh into the collective decision we have made. My brother has information on a King we know nothing about. A King who killed the Queen, and three Ceders, and more Affinites than I can name right now. He might have many other plans for which we can prepare if only we have some place to start. If the Small Council thinks the place to start is with my brother's memories, then that is where you start. I will pray that you can heal my brother along the way, but that is not your priority."

Olga Masalis was looking at Jackson, unmoved, as he spoke. Arnar Jakobsson was less good at hiding his emotions. He stared at Jackson in utter disbelief. But Olga knew Jackson; had worked with him after the war against Astaroth. She knew where his and Percy's loyalties lay. She knew every word he spoke was the truth.

At that moment, Dagmara and Bianka stepped out of the shack and, together with Jillian and Arthur, walked over to Jackson. "He is doing well," Bianka said. Dagmara remained quiet by her side. "We will have nurses monitor him, and there will be security for his safety. I am sorry it had to be this way."

Jackson smiled weakly at the Chief Medical Officer. "You saved his life. You have nothing to be sorry for."

Bianka nodded to Jackson, and then gestured to Dagmara to come with her. The two women headed down the path and vanished behind the cliffs. Arthur put a comforting arm around his cousin and he and Jillian turned to follow them back to the castle. At that moment Axel appeared again. The look on his face said enough.

"What's happened?" Jackson asked.

"They found Myat Kyu's body. It's highly likely that Rosanna Zambrano's will be found in the same vicinity." His voice was tight with emotion. He turned to Olga, his gaze unflinching. "Do you understand what this means? That man in there is the only lead we have on the new enemy we are facing in South America. You will do well to remember that you follow my orders. If you cannot get him to speak of his experience, the Ceders might soon be up against an enemy so elusive that they will not see him coming until it is too late. Perhaps the Asters will one day, too. Percy is not some regular patient, Doctor. I advise you to not treat him as such."

Chapter 11

The alarm was roaring in their ears as Sophie and Sky ran up the stairs that led back up to the grand entrance hall. They didn't have many weapons on them. The Disciple only had a single sword and a small dagger on him. Sophie now had the sword strapped to her back, while Sky led the way with the dagger in his hand.

They hadn't mentioned Lian since they had left their prison cell. Talking about it wouldn't do either of them any good. Instead, they had decided very quickly on how they were going to bring down Mitrik's castle. They didn't have Matu's strength to destroy the weight-bearing, marble pillars in the entrance hall. That would've been the fastest way to bring the core of the castle crumbling down.

So, they needed a different plan.

They had a different plan.

Luckily for them, Sophie had once spent hours in the library studying the floor plans of Mitrik's white castle. An elusive Merger by the name of Agatha Jones had sent back the detailed drawings of all the different rooms and passages. She was the most successful Merger in history, somehow gaining access to this stronghold without blowing her cover. Sophie wondered where she was now.

With a little help from her magic of memory, Sophie led the way back up to the main entrance hall with the helical staircase. Once they had broken through the trapdoor, there were five Disciples in the room.

They all carried the black weapons of Mitrik's foot soldiers.

Even though they were outnumbered, Sky and Sophie had no trouble bringing these Disciples down. Especially with Sky's speed and Sophie's clever moves, where she provoked exactly the attacks she expected, the five soldiers were down in less than a minute.

Sophie noted how deadly she and her brother were. There was no hesitation, only stone-cold brutality. As if neither she nor Sky felt anything as they fought. Sophie wondered if this was similar to what Nathan turned into on missions. All focus and no emotion. She couldn't let herself feel at this moment. If she would feel, she would lose control. Not like when Gayle died, but in such a way that she wouldn't be able to finish the task at hand.

They quickly stripped the Disciples of their weapons and strapped as many as they could to their own belts.

"This way." Sophie jumped up and ran around the helical staircase to the back of the entrance hall. She dashed through the double glass doors and found herself in the room she had expected to find; a large dining hall, with an immensely long wooden table in the middle. Sophie guessed at least a hundred people could be seated around it at one time.

Sophie scanned the room, and found a normal-sized door to her left, just where she knew it would be. She sprinted past the dining table and pulled open the door. There was a staircase on the other side that led down.

"You're sure?" Sky asked quickly. Sophie glanced over her shoulder, but before she could answer her brother, the double glass entrance doors behind him were thrown open and a group of six Disciples burst in.

"Never mind." Sky pushed her through the doorway with one hand and slammed the door shut behind them with the other.

Sophie threw herself down the wooden staircase as fast as she could go, her eyes on the steps beneath her feet to keep herself from falling.

They reached the bottom of the winding staircase and were met with another closed door. Sophie pushed against it, and it flew open. The two Asters found themselves in the castle kitchens. It was the same size as the dining room far above them, with counters and cabinets lining all four walls, and a gigantic island with large stoves in the centre of the room. Metal pots and pans hung from the ceiling, and the counters were covered with modern kitchen appliances. Unlike the rest of the castle, the entire kitchen was made of stainless steel.

The second they entered, Sophie and Sky immediately commenced battle with the Disciple chefs inside. The chefs weren't fighters and they didn't have proper weapons, but they didn't hesitate to reach for the kitchen knives.

Sophie dug into her magic and advanced on her two chef attackers with the precise knowledge of how to read their attacks right before they would come. She saw every blow coming, and met every attack with one of her own. With all her pent-up rage from what had happened to Lian, her blows were stronger than ever before.

These Disciples weren't fighters, but they were good at using whatever objects they had at their disposal. When Sophie brought down her sword, which caused one Disciple to drop her large kitchen knife, and Sophie was about to deliver the blow that would kill, the chef had turned around and blocked the attack with a frying pan.

Still, it wasn't enough to keep them alive.

There was a thundering of footsteps coming down the staircase that led to the dining room. Sky shot over to the door immediately, and managed to throw the bolts over to lock it.

"We need to buy some time!" Sky called to Sophie.

"On it!" Sophie called back. She was already going through the pockets of all the dead chefs. Sky grunted from the door as he pressed his body against the wood to keep it closed.

"Jackpot," Sophie gasped as she found a key in one of the chef's pockets. "Try this!"

Sophie tossed the key over to Sky and he tried the key in the lock. It made a satisfying locking sound. Blowing out a breath of relief, Sky stepped away from the door.

"That won't hold them for long," Sky said. They could both hear the Disciples on the other side throwing their weight against the door. The wood creaked a little louder each time they did so.

"Help me with the fridge," Sophie said. There was a gigantic double-door fridge next to the door, and Sophie and Sky pushed and pulled it in such a way that it toppled onto its side right in front of the door. The damn thing was heavy enough that they should have enough time now to get what they came here for.

"Grab everything you can find. There are cooking oils by the stoves and there must be alcohol here somewhere, maybe even a blowtorch," Sophie said.

Sky stared at her blankly.

Sophie stopped for a moment to look at him. "Yes, people use blowtorches when cooking," she said sardonically, before moving through the kitchen and throwing open every cupboard she passed.

Sky didn't reply. He headed for the stoves while Sophie made her way through the closed wooden cabinets hanging along the walls. She pulled them all open. Most of them were filled with tinned food, but she found the drinks cabinet soon enough, with boxes of alcohol bottles stacked five deep per shelf.

Sophie pulled out the boxes labelled brandy and placed them in the middle of the kitchen. The Disciples were still trying to force their way through the door, but the toppled fridge was holding steady.

After they had gathered all the flammable liquids into one pile, Sophie knelt near it. There were seven boxes that contained six bottles of brandy each, and Sky had found another six bottles of cooking oil, and with an attempted smile, but what looked more like a grimace, he produced two blowtorches, too. Sophie gave him a single nod. She took one from him and hooked it onto her belt; Sky did the same.

"You can shimmer all of this to the entrance hall?" Sophie asked.

Sky nodded. "Where do you want them?"

"Under the staircase."

Sky held out his bloodied hand to Sophie. She took it without hesitation. Even through the banging against the door held closed by the fridge, and the alarm ringing through the whole castle, Sophie found that part of herself that could make everything external fade into the background.

Sky held his free hand above the pile of alcohol and cooking oils and closed his eyes. It took another second for him to concentrate, but soon enough a blue light surrounded them, and they vanished from the castle's kitchens. When they appeared again, they were kneeling underneath the glass, helical staircase in the entrance hall.

The two Asters jumped to their feet immediately, because three running Disciples had caught sight of their sudden appearance and attacked them.

They were dead in seconds.

"Grab what you can carry and follow me," Sophie said. She pulled out two bottles of brandy, holding one in each hand, and started running up the staircase. Sky followed suit and was right behind her. When they reached the first floor, Sophie didn't slow down. She continued up the staircase, all the way up to the sixth floor. It was only near the top that they met any more Disciples, who stepped onto the staircase after coming out of a nearby door on the fifth floor.

The element of surprise was all Sophie needed. She swung one of the brandy bottles and hit one Disciple right across the side of his head. The bottle shattered, splashing liquor all around them. Sophie turned away immediately and did the same thing with the next Disciple. There was a blue flash speeding all around her, as Sky took on the other Disciples with his bottles of brandy, breaking them, too, and then reaching for his weapons to finish the job.

Sophie pulled her sword back out from its sheath on her back and jumped down a few steps to avoid another blow. She sliced her sword across the shins of the Disciple looming over her; he was standing a few steps higher on the staircase. The Disciple cried out, and his stumble was enough for Sophie to jump up and jam a knife through his heart.

When she pulled the knife back out, she found all eight Disciples now dead on the stairs. Spilled liquor mingled with blood flowed on down the stairs. It was a sickly combination.

"We're out of brandy," Sky said, panting. He sheathed his weapons once again.

"Why did you think I had you shimmer the rest underneath the staircase?" Sophie asked. She pointed down. The helical, glass staircase was so clear that, even six floors down, they could see the pile of brandy and cooking oils all the way at the bottom. Sophie looked up and found Sky smiling to himself, if only momentarily.

"Shimmer some up," Sophie said.

Sky looked down and the Band on his wrist started glowing. A blue flash appeared, and when it vanished, there was a bottle of brandy in each hand. Sky passed the bottles to Sophie before doing the same thing once more.

"Okay, come on," Sophie said. She stepped onto the landing of the sixth floor, unscrewed the tops of the brandy bottles and started pouring the contents all across the landing, all over the furnishings. They opened some of the closed doors and poured some in there as well, making sure the pools of liquid were all connected.

Sophie could hear more running footsteps on the stairs below them, but she didn't care. She knew this was going to work, and she knew no Disciple was strong enough to kill them. Not now. Sophie wouldn't let anybody else die.

She knew Sky felt the same.

"We need to do this on each floor," she told Sky as he used his magic to shimmer more bottles to them so that they could soak the heart of Mitrik's main castle from top to bottom. They headed down to the fifth floor.

"And then—" Sophie started, but her smashing another bottle and soaking a long rug stopped her mid-sentence. When she re-joined Sky at the staircase, he finished for her.

"And then we have the whole place go up in flames."

Chapter 12

It had taken all morning and part of that afternoon, but Nathan, Matu and Lian had finally made it to the marble path that led to the white castle. They'd barely had any trouble along the way. The day before, they'd grabbed a single Disciple, and with a knife at her back, the woman had led them a good chunk of the way to Mitrik's castle. The Asters had killed her and hidden her body in another discarded room in the tunnels. Very early the next morning they'd done the same to a male Disciple, who had led them straight to the white and iron door. They'd killed him, too, and tossed him into the depths of the chasm on the side of the marble path.

The three boys couldn't run down the path; they couldn't arouse too much suspicion. They'd managed to get this far without detection and they weren't planning on blowing their cover now. Not when they were so close.

They were about three quarters of the way down the marble path when the alarm went off. The booming sound echoed off the walls of the cavern. It sounded similar to the one that had gone off when Mitrik had exposed their arrival in the Underworld. All three Asters froze for a moment, ready for if the alarm signalled *their* presence.

But the other Disciples on the path paid no attention to them. Instead, they had all started running towards the castle.

"Come on," Matu said, and he joined the other Disciples as they ran.

Whatever the alarm meant, it was useful because the Asters could now get to the white castle a whole lot faster without drawing any attention to themselves.

Nathan cast a glance behind him, and found that no new Disciples were coming in through the iron door and heading down the path. He didn't stop to wonder why; finding Sophie and Sky was his focus now.

The three boys dashed across the drawbridge and onto the white cobblestone streets. They raced up the steps, past the battlements. As he ran, Nathan realised that many Disciples were now running away from the castle, rather than towards it. Most of them weren't in armour and didn't carry any weapons at all. He'd almost forgotten that not all Disciples were warriors, just like not all Affinites were soldiers. They all had their own affinities, which for the most part defined what they would be in life. Some of these fleeing Disciples could just be involved in running the castle.

Matu was in front. He told them not to touch any Disciple that rushed past them in the other direction. Nathan hadn't planned on doing so. These Disciples were obviously no threat to them or to Sophie and Sky. They could just be left alone.

Matu led the way up the white cobblestone path until the white iron gates that led towards the castle's main entrance came into view. There were four Disciples standing guard. Two of them had their backs towards the path and were looking up through the gate to the entrance of the castle. The other two were watching every Disciple that shot past them and away down the path.

"We need to be in front," Nathan said. The white bone weapons he and Lian were carrying might just be enough to get them through the gates without much trouble.

Matu grunted his acknowledgment and let both of them pass him.

The guards, who only had black weapons, took one look at the white daggers and nodded to Nathan and Lian. They stepped aside, pulling open the iron gates with them. Nathan and Lian stepped past the guards with ease, but when Matu tried to do the same, the two guards held up their hands in front of him, blocking his way.

"Not you. You are not trained," the one on the right grumbled. He wouldn't live long enough to regret it. There was a flash of iron and black and bone white and all four guards were lying dead on the ground. They might have expected resistance from Matu, who'd they'd refused entrance, but they hadn't expected Lian and Nathan to join in the fight from behind them. The Asters quickly disposed of the bodies in the guard house and deliberately closed the iron gate so none of the fleeing Disciples would attempt to exit the castle there and question the absence of the guards.

Nathan led the way up the final steps to the two stories-tall, main door to the castle. Right before they reached it, there was a loud explosion behind them.

All three of them turned around. The sound had come from the distance, probably close to the rock wall of the enormous cavern. Nathan couldn't tell where exactly it had come from, but it hadn't sounded good.

"What the hell was that?" Lian gasped.

"No idea," Matu muttered.

"Not now," Nathan snapped.

They couldn't worry about that right now. They needed to find Sophie and Sky and then get the hell out of there.

The boys turned back to the door. Lian pulled it open and they dashed into the main entrance hall.

The very first thing Nathan noticed was that, oddly, there were boxes underneath the magnificent, glass, helical staircase in the middle of the hall. Some of the boxes had bottles of brandy in them, and some were completely empty. And before any of them could pick a direction as to where to start their search, they heard the sounds of a struggle just above them.

Seconds later, a Disciple body fell down the stairs. And then...

"LIAN!"

In a flurry of blonde hair, Sophie slammed into Lian and threw her arms around him. Lian, in turn, stumbled back in a state of confusion, barely keeping his footing at the force of Sophie's impact.

Nathan stared at the two of them in bewilderment. He then turned his head to the helical staircase and found Sky standing on the bottom step, his mouth hanging open in shock. His eyes were so wide as he stared at Lian as well. He didn't seem to be able to move.

Sophie still had her arms around Lian and was gabbling out a string of words. Lian had closed his arms around her, as well, and had started soothing her. He still had a confused look on his face; not entirely understanding Sophie's reaction.

At a certain point, Lian pulled his arms back and asked kindly, "What's going on?"

Sophie loosened her arms and took a step back. It was only then that Nathan saw that she was crying. Some distant, faraway part of him tried to urge him to step forward and provide comfort, but an icy layer inside of him stopped him from moving. Now was not the time, it was saying. Now only the mission was important; the task at hand.

"We thought you were dead. Sky heard your voice; he heard you die," Sophie sobbed.

Understanding filled Lian's eyes. Nathan didn't know how many times Lian had called Sky. Matu had called Sky as well. Because neither of them got a response, no one thought Sky had actually heard them.

"I'm so sorry. But I'm okay. Nate saved me just in time. He had his vines keep me alive from a distance so they had time to find me," Lian said in a calming voice.

Sophie looked away from Lian and over to Nathan. "You did that?" she asked quietly.

By the way she was looking at him, Nathan didn't quite know how to respond. He opted for a short nod, and not to say anything. He hadn't expected any further response from Sophie, but she stepped towards him, and hugged him as well.

"Thank you," she whispered as she tightened her arms around him.

Completely stunned, Nathan did nothing other than close his arms around her as well. There was something strange about the situation. They'd never got so emotional on a mission before. There was something conflicting about it.

Over Sophie's shoulder, Nathan caught how Sky moved from his spot on the staircase, and was slowly moving towards Lian. His whole face was open; there was no cocky façade that hid what Sky felt underneath. He'd heard Lian dying; his best friend, his brother. His annoying twin, as Matu sometimes referred to them.

A few feet in front of Lian, Sky stopped. He stared at his brother. He reached out and gripped Lian's shoulder. Lian, in turn, looked at Sky and nodded.

"I'm okay," he said softly.

Sky squeezed Lian's shoulder more tightly, nodded, and then let go.

At that moment, Sophie let go of Nathan. She wiped the tears from her face and turned to the others. It was time they got back to business.

"What were you guys doing?" Matu asked.

Sky chuckled and looked over to Sophie. "We were going to burn the castle to the ground."

"We thought if we could bring down the castle, it would send a message and scatter Mitrik's following," Sophie added. "Mitrik's not here."

"We know," Lian said.

"We still might face other inner circle members, though," Matu pointed out.

"Most Disciples have already left this part of the castle," Sky said.

"And even if we do meet any, we really only have to worry about Kali,"

Sophie added.

"Kali?" Nathan asked.

"Mitrik's third-in-command. His Second went with him. Kali is dangerous; she's stronger and faster than any Disciple should be," Sophie explained. She looked quickly at Lian, nodded to herself, and then turned her attention back to the task at hand. "But that doesn't matter right now. The brandy will only make a superficial fire. The castle is mostly stone so it will take some time to burn the whole place down."

"Then we tear it down as well," Matu decided.

Sky headed over to the boxes under the stairs and grabbed the final brandy bottles. He unscrewed them and splashed the liquor all over the carpets covering the floor of the entrance hall. As he did so, Nathan studied the marble pillars of the entrance hall. They held up the entire weight of the core of the castle.

"We need to do all of it at the same time; the fire, the breaking, the shimmering out," Sophie said.

"I can help with that," Nathan said. He pointed at the pillars. They were half built into the walls of the entrance hall. Nathan then looked at Sophie with a question in his eyes. He knew she'd studied the blueprints of the white castle. She'd know what he was asking.

Sophie turned to the pillars and pointed at six in particular. "Those are weight-bearing."

Nathan nodded and held up his hands. The Band on his wrist started glowing green as his magic soared through his body. The outer layer of the pillars started cracking and breaking free. First, little green tips appeared, but it didn't take long before thick, green vines appeared and started snaking around the weight-bearing pillars. One part of each vine grew longer and longer and headed towards where Nathan was standing, while the other parts kept wrapping themselves around each pillar, until they covered at least three feet.

Then the loose ends of the vines snaked past Nathan to reach Matu. Nathan looked over his shoulder and his Band stopped glowing. Matu knew exactly what was expected of him. He grabbed all ends of the vines and wrapped them around his hands and wrists for better grip.

Matu's Band started glowing a deep bronze.

"Ready," he said.

Even though Sky said this part of the castle was deserted, they could hear running footsteps coming from the stairs a few levels above them. Then Nathan noticed that there were also footsteps coming from the room behind the helical staircase as well.

"They're coming," Lian warned.

"They'll be too late," Sky said. He and Sophie positioned themselves at the edge of the liquor pool, took the blowtorches from their belts and fired them up.

"What the..." Lian started to say.

Sophie grinned over her shoulder. "It's called flaming. It's used for caramelisation!"

Lian stared at her, bewildered once again.

"Not now, Sherlock!" Sky called.

Sophie grinned at her brother. He smiled back at her.

"Guys..." Matu grumbled.

Sophie looked over her shoulder. "We're ready," she said.

From one moment to the next, Matu threw all of his magic into his body and pulled with all his might on the vines around the pillars. There was a great rumble and crack, and the vines, with the section of the pillar they had wrapped themselves around, broke loose. Immense cracks appeared along the walls, and the whole castle seemed to moan.

Then great blocks of stone and bits of plaster started raining down from the ceiling as the pillars broke, and no longer held the weight of the castle's core above them.

"Now!" Sky called.

He and Sophie angled the blowtorches to the liquor, igniting the alcohol and oil covering the floor. The flames took hold quickly, flaring up everywhere the brandy and oil had been splashed on the ground. The fire burned bright and sped up the helical staircase.

They didn't have time to see the fire erupting out on the upper floors. The castle was about to fall down on top of them. Sky and Sophie spun around and raced the few feet towards Matu. Lian and Nathan were already there. The second they held on to each other, blue light appeared, and the ground vanished underneath their feet.

Nathan had the vague feeling of flying. He could feel the air brush against his face as they flew through space away from Mitrik's castle. He didn't know exactly where Sky was shimmering them to, but Nathan was expecting to feel the rocky ground of the *Angel Trail* underneath his feet any moment now.

But that soft landing and the feeling of firm ground underneath his feet never came. Instead, he felt like one moment he was flying through the air and the next he had crashed against an invisible wall. Something similar to an electric shock seemed to shoot through his body as he felt himself tumble down... and even further down.

Nathan still couldn't see anything. There was only the blue light that filled his vision, but he was very aware that something was going wrong. A horrible sensation in his stomach told him he was falling. He couldn't manage to keep a hold of Sophie and Matu as he fell further and further down until...

He landed on the ground with a thump. All the air got knocked out of his lungs. The blue light vanished from his sight, but it took him a long moment, while coughing, before he could see anything again. He was looking down, and realised that he wasn't lying on the rocky Canyon ground of the *Angel Trail*. He was lying on a marble path.

Nathan pushed himself up gingerly and saw that his Band was flickering. He could feel a sizzle go through his body from whatever that electric shock had been. He wasn't using his magic at all, and still his Band continued to flicker.

"No, no, no," Nathan heard behind him. He turned his head to find Sky sitting on his heels a few feet away from him. He was staring at his wrist where his Band was flickering dimly as well. Nathan looked further around and found that Matu and Sophie were on Sky's other side, also blinking and getting up carefully. Their Bands, too, were flickering. Nathan turned his head and found Lian on his other side.

Nathan pushed himself up onto his feet and swayed slightly. He looked around and realised they were standing on the marble path outside of the castle. They were close to the set of stairs near the white and iron door that led to the Underworld tunnels beyond. They hadn't made it outside. They weren't even out of Mitrik's cavern.

"What happened?" Sophie asked.

"Something blocked me," Sky answered. He had got to his feet and took a staggering step towards the staircase. "I am getting so tired of these bloody veils!" he shouted angrily.

"But we came through here no problem," Matu said.

"Some veils can be made one way. They'll let you in, but they won't let you out," Sky snapped.

Lian frowned. "How would you know that?"

Sky glared at his brother. Nathan didn't understand the anger. He didn't understand what point it had. They needed to leave. They needed to find out a way to get through the veil. Anger wouldn't help. Emotion wouldn't help.

"Our prison was the same," Sophie whispered.

"Matu broke through the veil outside," Nathan said matter-of-factly.

Sophie nodded. "We just need to find out where the veil is." She headed for the stairs. She passed Lian, who was standing closest to the stairs. Lian made no move to follow her. He was rubbing the side of his arm, and frowning.

"What's wrong?" Matu asked.

"Something's wrong with my magic," Lian said. "I can feel the bruise."

Nathan turned away from him and focused on his magic. On the magic that he'd used only minutes ago to grow the vines that took down the castle's core. But there was nothing. No connection; nothing he could control and morph. He couldn't reach the magic within him. The feeling felt incredibly foreign.

"He's right," he said. "I can't grow vines."

"It's got to have something to do with when we crashed against the veil," Matu said.

"Which means even if we find it, you don't have the magic to break it?" Lian asked.

Matu swore in Swahili.

Running footsteps on the stairs made Nathan turn around. Sophie ran down, her eyes wide with shock. "We have a problem," she announced.

"Yes, we know. Our magic doesn't work from our crash against the veil," Sky snapped. Nathan could tell Sky was still trying to use his magic. It wasn't working, and it was making Sky even angrier.

"That's not the only thing," Sophie said. "The end of the path is gone. We can't get to the door, and I bet you that's where the veil starts."

"*What?*" Sky spat.

"It's crumbled away. Even with our magic, we can't reach the veil to break it. We can't get out this way," Sophie said. Her eyes darted all around as she sought out a new escape route. She even looked over the edge of the marble path into the chasm below.

The explosion... Nathan, Matu and Lian had heard an explosion right before they entered the white castle. That must've been to destroy the last part of the path so they couldn't get out. Mitrik might not be a fighter, and he might not even be here, but he was smart enough to leave behind a failsafe if Sophie and Sky managed to break out of their cell. He wasn't going to let anything jeopardise his possible alliance with the South American King.

"There is one other path that leads away from the castle," Matu said, pointing. To the left of the white castle in the distance, another, similar, path as the one they were on, snaked away to the left towards another great door in the cavern wall.

"It will be crawling with Disciples," Lian pointed out.

"It's the only way out we've got," Sky interrupted.

"I don't think we'll make it that far," Nathan said with a deadly calm. All his siblings were looking for other pathways to get out. They weren't even looking at the path they were on now. The four other Asters turned at his words.

Thirty feet away from them stood twenty Disciples. They were all wearing armour, and their bone-white weapons gleamed in their hands. And right in front stood a woman whose aura was almost tangible. She had a thick blonde-grey braid that hung over the front of her shoulder. Her sharp, pale, grey eyes were gloating in anticipation.

Somehow Nathan knew the woman in front was Kali, the Disciple Sophie warned them about, and Mitrik's third-in-command. Nathan remembered what Sophie had said about her. How she was different from the rest; faster, smarter, and had more power somehow. As if whatever affinity she possessed was amplified.

Nathan reached for the broadsword at his back. He sensed his brothers and sister readying themselves with their weapons, too. They might be without their magic, and even though they were outnumbered by inner circle soldiers, the Asters were still a force to be reckoned with. The only unknown factor was the woman in front.

Kali grinned a terrifying grin as she stepped forward, away from the rest of Mitrik's inner circle, and said, "You're right, boy. You *won't* make it that far."

Chapter 13

The marble path was only a few feet wide. A maximum of three people could stand next to each other without falling off. Matu and Sky took up position in front while Nathan, Sophie and Lian stood behind them. Sophie glanced at her wrist for a brief moment and found that her Band was still flickering.

Her magic still wasn't working.

No Disciple made it into a King's inner circle without being an extremely good fighter or a genius strategist. Sophie's heart hammered in her chest as she took in all the Disciples and their brighter-than-white weapons. Though, none of the other nineteen Disciples scared Sophie as much as Kali did. The King's third-in-command wasn't armoured with a multitude of swords and daggers like the others. She had her one white dagger at her waist, but her hands weren't anywhere near it. Unlike any Disciple Sophie had ever encountered, Kali had two whips coiled around each of her shoulders. She'd had them when Sophie and Sky were first taken prisoner, but now she was purposefully holding their handles with the kind of ease that came with long use.

Kali broke further away from the other nineteen Disciples and stepped towards the Asters. She was still wearing the thick, black make-up around her eyes, which made her pale grey eyes stand out. They weren't like Mitrik's liquid silver eyes, but they were equally unnerving. Sophie could *feel* Kali's aura as she stepped closer to them.

"It was a smart plan," Kali said, her voice cold. "But not smart enough. It is clear you have only ever encountered soldiers. Even in his absence, Mitrik made sure you could never leave. And without your little powers to help you... Well..."

Kali flashed a wolfish grin. Behind her, the other Disciples remained unmoved, their faces stonily neutral as they waited for their Commander to give them orders. Kali was closer to the Asters now than she was to her subordinates, but she showed not a single trace of nerves.

Sophie reached for the sword at her back. In front of her, Matu and Sky had their hands on their weapons. The chances were slim that they would get out of this alive. Without their magic and with nowhere to run... But Sophie had briefly experienced what it felt like to lose one of her siblings. Now that it turned out not to be true, she would give Kali and her crew a damn good run for their money before she'd let anything happen to her family.

Sophie turned her head and met Nathan's gaze. There was something comforting about the cold focus in his eyes; that icy fire that told her he would fight to the very end with her. His short nod to her only confirmed that.

Even if they didn't all make it out, Sophie hoped that their destruction of the castle was enough to scatter Mitrik's rebellion outside. The destruction of his strongest base might be enough for his followers to lose faith in him. That had been their mission: to quell the rebellion. Now wasn't the time to think about there being a larger threat to the Affinites and humans still to come if Mitrik succeeded in his alliance with the South American King.

Far behind the Disciples, the white castle was burning and collapsing in on itself.

Sophie breathed in and out slowly, stilling her body, preparing for battle.

Kali stopped a mere ten feet away from Sky and Matu. They wouldn't attack her. She held all the power in this situation. Their only hope of all of them surviving this, was if they would be taken out alive, as prisoners. Though, by the looks on the Disciple's faces, Sophie knew enough about their intentions.

They were here to kill.

The King who killed not one, but all the Asters. Mitrik would go down in history. Maybe he had planned this all along. Or maybe he didn't realise that his failsafe was a better plan than his original one of showing Sky and Sophie off to the South American King. Sophie didn't know what to think anymore. The North American King had almost become as much of a mystery to her as the South American one.

Kali moved her hands and pulled the coiled whips free. They uncurled on the marble path, rippling like deadly snakes. She turned sideways and made sure the whips were free from each other in front of her. These whips were unlike anything Sophie had ever seen before. They were sharp; edged with metal. All it would take was one small twist of her wrists, and Kali could cut two of them in half at the same time. She was just far enough away, so that the Asters couldn't even hope to stop her attack. And yet she was close enough to land a killing blow with one of those metallic whips.

Kali looked down in front of her, over the edge of the path. "You know, no one knows the true depths of these chasms," she said chillingly, her meaning clear. She didn't look at them as she spoke in her cold, unfeeling voice. There was also no amusement there, unlike what Sophie had become accustomed to when Disciples thought that they had managed to push an Aster into a corner.

"These chasms strike fear in everyone who walks along this path. I've been here long enough to know that the chasms are the King's favourite method of execution. That and the fighting rings, of course," Kali continued.

Sophie wondered why she was saying all of this. It was only giving the Asters more time for their magic to come back to them. And yet Kali was taking her time, enjoying her moment of supremacy. She had transferred the handles of the two whips to one hand and was stretching and twisting the other, as if she was warming it up before attacking. She took a whip in each hand again and tightened her grip.

"The King makes sure the fall comes as a surprise. It's the fear of everyone who walks here; not knowing if they might be thrown in." Kali glanced at them slyly. "Though, you all might be pretty well prepared now." She cocked her head. "Yet, maybe some here aren't."

Kali flashed another deadly grin and raised her hands, the whips rising with her. In unison, the five Asters set themselves for their deadly impact.

In a flash, Kali twisted her body and brought the whips down. In a snap, the long, metallic whips followed the movement of Kali's arms. It was unlike anything Sophie had ever seen before. There was a crackle of energy as Kali brought her arms down. Sparks of purple light erupted from Kali's hands and followed each whip's wave as it extended from her hands right down to the tip. But the magic-like sparks weren't the only thing that moved along with the whip. The marble path underneath their feet cracked open as the whole thing moved upwards with the wave of the two whips. The marble surface crumbled and broke apart as the entire path, with all the rock underneath it, moved as a wave in synchrony with the whips.

The grumble and shake of the marble path was enough for the Asters to lose their footing. As one, they crouched low to the ground to maintain balance, bracing themselves for the impact of the wave and its dreadful aftermath; that long fall down into the chasm.

But the impact never came.

Barely believing their eyes, the Asters watched, dazed, as the wave of the path, and the snap of the whips and the angle of Kali's attack, wasn't coming their way; it was headed in the other direction.

She hadn't turned towards the Asters. She had turned towards the other nineteen Disciples from Mitrik's inner circle.

The whips weren't long enough to reach to the first line of Disciples, but the wave of the path was much more dangerous. With the speed of Kali's snapping whips, and the energy that almost looked like magic, the entire path rose up with the arch of the whips, and a wave of marble and ancient rock rumbled towards the Disciples.

They were taken completely unaware.

The moment the wave reached them, the Disciples were thrown off their feet and into the air. The majority was flung to the side and fell, screaming in shock and fear, into the depths of the chasm below.

A few Disciples landed back on the path, but Kali was already there, dagger in hand. She shot forward towards them, and spun, jumped and darted in between the Disciples still alive. She stabbed and sliced with her single bone-white dagger, not giving any Disciple the chance to get to their feet to fight her properly.

Not that they could get to their feet. The marble path was still following its wave-like movement all the way down to the drawbridge at the bottom of the white castle. The path that remained behind didn't still, either. It rumbled and it cracked and it shuddered. Sophie was amazed at how Kali was able to keep her footing as more cracks appeared and part of the path moved, broke and fell away.

Kali cast a look over her shoulder. "Come on!" she shouted at the five Asters, who, while also trying to keep their balance and not fall into the chasm, stood almost frozen in bewilderment at what had just happened.

Kali's shout brought them all back to reality, and they shot forward. They jumped and stumbled down the path, back towards the castle. It shuddered and shook and trembled. Parts of the path broke away and Sophie had to jump over an open space almost five feet wide to get to the other side.

She didn't have time to process what had just happened. Who the hell was this woman who was running out in front of them? Who had just saved their lives? Who was somehow Mitrik's *third-in-command*? Kali had wielded an energy that no Disciple should be able to command. As Sophie thought about it, no Affinite would be able to, either.

It was like magic. And yet it wasn't.

"Who are you?" Sophie shouted up ahead. She then gasped as another part of the path broke away in front of her. The very ground beneath her feet was shaking, and she could barely stay on her feet. Matu and Kali were already on the other side. Both of them had turned around and were beckoning for her to jump.

Sophie didn't have time to think. She swallowed once and leaped.

She only just made it to the other side, landing painfully on her knees. A second later two sets of hands were heaving her back onto her feet.

"Go!" Matu shouted.

Sophie and Kali didn't think twice. Matu would help the other boys get across. They needed to get off this path as soon as possible.

As the two of them ran, stumbling along the way, Kali said, in between pants, "My name—is Agatha Jones."

If Sophie could stop and stare at the woman next to her, she would have. Agatha Jones' name was almost mythic, though Sophie always knew she was real. She'd studied the hundreds of detailed maps Saluverus' most successful Merger, and one and only Indigo, had sent to the Small Council.

An Indigo was rare. Incredibly rare. They came along maybe once in a generation. An Indigo was born from two Affinite parents, like many regular Affinites were. But instead of inheriting a single affinity from one of the two parents, an Indigo inherited both. The amalgamation of the two affinities leads to a crackle of raw energy that borders on the same kind of energy found in magic. An Indigo could harness that energy in small bursts of light, heat or electricity.

Agatha Jones was a legend. Sophie didn't know much about her, except that her father had been one of Glacialis' scientists, and that she possessed the affinities of survival and intelligence. The second she was allowed to go undercover and become a Merger, she did. She never resurfaced.

Behind Sophie, her brothers were starting to catch up. The entire chasm was filled with the deafening noise of fallen masonry. The castle up in front of them was collapsing, sending a roaring echo through the space. And the collapse of the marble path caused deadening booms, deep groans and rumbles, and crashes.

"You could have reported Mitrik's plans sooner!" Sky called up to Agatha. He was right behind the two girls now. If they weren't about to fall, Sophie would have turned around to kick him. There were so many things she wanted to talk to Agatha about; accusing her of not reporting Mitrik's uprising wasn't one of them.

A crack appeared right where Sophie was about to put down her foot. She managed to just avoid it, but the whole path groaned and shook, and she stumbled. Pain shot through her as she once more landed on her knees.

There was no time to think. Sophie jumped up again and raced on. The whole cavern seemed to be moaning now. Rocks from the ceiling were falling down as well. One barely missed Agatha, who was still running up ahead. Sophie doubted even Agatha knew her explosion of energy would've caused this.

There was a roaring in Sophie's ears. She couldn't even hear her brothers behind her. Just once she dared to look over her shoulder to see if they were still there.

"Keep your eyes forward!" Nathan snapped at her. He and Matu were running behind Sky, while Lian took up the rear. Lian, Sophie saw, had an extremely worried look on his face. All their Bands were still flickering. Sophie couldn't imagine what Lian must be feeling. Well, she could. She could still feel the bruising of her knees from when she stumbled. Lian's magic prevented him from even feeling that. Right now, he was focusing so hard, probably trying to ignore what he hadn't felt in years.

Sophie concentrated on the Indigo in front of her. Agatha had almost reached the drawbridge. But instead of heading straight towards it, she veered to the right and jumped off the path altogether.

Sophie slowed slightly, shocked at Agatha's sudden leap into the darkness below.

"Come on!" Sky shouted. As he passed her, he caught her arm and dragged her behind him. Sophie quickly matched his speed. He was just up ahead of her, and they were nearing the place where Agatha jumped.

Sky didn't even think about it, and jumped.

Sophie swallowed once and readied herself.

For a brief moment as she fell, she was enveloped in darkness, not knowing what she would meet at the bottom.

Her landing was softer than she expected. Though, the impact still shuddered through her entire body. Sophie couldn't register what she had fallen on. There was no time.

"Get up!" Agatha shouted. As Sophie made to get to her feet, an arm grabbed her and yanked her up the rest of the way. When she stood, Agatha put a hand to her back and pushed her into a dimly lit tunnel.

There were a few lanterns on the walls, but they were shaking considerably. Rocks were falling from the ceiling, and Sophie thought there was a bigger chance of them being buried alive than getting out of there. Especially with their magic still not working.

"You'll reach the veil! Your magic should be coming back soon!" Agatha shouted. "GO!"

There were so many things Sophie wanted to say; wanted to ask. But there was no time. Lian had already landed and was right behind her. Ahead of her, Sophie could just make out Sky's receding form. She shot forward into the darkened tunnel. The whole thing shook and groaned, but at least the ground was steady underneath her feet here. She only needed to focus on the rocks falling down from the low ceiling.

Then Sophie slowed. She suddenly had a bad feeling.

"Soph, keep going!" Lian shouted as he passed her.

"What about Agatha?" Sophie shouted back. She held her hands over her head and jumped out of the way of quite a large rock breaking free from the ceiling.

Dust flew in through the tunnel from where they'd come from. A great crash sounded from there as well.

Then Matu and Nathan dashed into view. But there was no one behind them.

"Where is she?" Sophie shouted.

"Not now!" Matu told her.

Sophie glanced back once more before running after her brothers. Agatha hadn't come with them. Why?

As she ran, Sophie could barely see where she was going. She jumped over a lantern that had fallen to the ground. She held her hands in front of her eyes to shield them from the dust, but it was no use. The ceiling started cracking above her. Great, big tears were forming, and Sophie knew it wouldn't be long before the entire tunnel caved in. She could hear the booms and rumbling of the tunnel collapsing behind her.

Sophie ran as fast as she could. Suddenly she felt a tingling in her wrist. She looked down and saw that her Band was no longer flickering; it was glowing strongly.

A wave of relief went through her.

Her magic was back. Agatha had been right.

Up ahead she could see shadows through the dust. Her brothers had come to a standstill. Sophie met them and saw that Matu was up front. His Band was glowing a fierce bronze as he pulled his arm back and threw all his strength into a single punch.

There was a loud bang.

Matu didn't move forward. He pulled his hand back and swung again.

There was another bang.

Sophie looked behind her worryingly. The great rumbling was coming closer. It was like a tsunami of rock and debris and dust that was heading their way.

Another bang.

And then a flash of white light and the sound of the veil shattering.

Matu moved. The other Asters followed. They hurried a few feet further so that they could all pass through the broken shards of the veil to the other side.

"Hold on!" Sky called out over the thundering noise of the tunnel breaking apart behind them. Sophie grabbed the two brothers closest to her; not even a second passed before a blue flash appeared and they shimmered out of the tunnel, out of Mitrik's cavern, and back out into the Grand Canyon.

Chances were, they would meet a small army of Disciples who would be furious that they had destroyed their capital castle, and the entire cavern along with it.

Sophie sucked in her breath and prepared for the worst.

Chapter 14

When the blue light of Sky's shimmer vanished, the five Asters found themselves up on the *Angel Trail*. Sky had chosen this position because he didn't think shimmering too close to the entrance of the Underworld would be the smartest thing to do. Especially since they didn't know what the situation outside would be.

Even then, Sky expected there to be Disciples around. Since there were still humans down there somewhere in need of saving, the Disciples could be laying out a trap. To his surprise, however, there was no one on the trail, and no army waiting for them at the bottom.

The first thing Sky noticed was the black smoke that was rising up from the Canyon floor. He peered over the edge of the trail and found that the largest circus-like tent had been set on fire. The moment he saw this, he heard the helicopter.

Sky looked up. The black helicopter was too far away from them to see who was piloting it, but there was a logo on its side, a single brown triangle with a yellow sun around its tip; David Hughes' logo.

The helicopter was larger than any Sky had ever seen before. It was longer than the standard type, with three windows behind the cockpit, instead of the usual one or two. The helicopter flew straight over their heads, and as it passed over the smaller tents around the circus tent, a large object was tossed out from its side. Sky's eyes followed the object down, and where it landed, it burst into flames, causing the nearby tents to catch fire.

"Well, that's one way of scattering the Disciples," Lian commented.

Sky looked along the Canyon floor and saw what Lian meant.

"They're all leaving," Matu observed. A whole company of Disciples was on their horses, rushing away from the fire. The camp already looked empty, as if half of the Disciples had packed everything up before David Hughes even arrived. The Disciples that hadn't left yet were rushing from their tents, clutching bags and running down alongside the river snaking in between the Canyon walls.

"Why didn't Agatha come with us?" Sophie asked.

"She said she had to stay," Matu said.

"You couldn't convince her to come? What if she couldn't get out in time?" Sophie asked.

"We tried, but it was already too late. She was trying to tell us something when the ceiling came down in between us," Matu explained.

"Any idea what she wanted to say?" Lian asked.

Matu shook his head. "Something about Mitrik, is my guess."

"Look," Nathan said, pointing down. They all followed the line of Nathan's finger. In the middle of the camp, by the river, stood three Disciples with bone-white weapons. They were discussing something, pointing towards the horde of Disciples fleeing the camp, and then the helicopter above setting fire to the main tents. They didn't seem angry that the camp was leaving; they weren't ordering anyone to stay. Sky remembered Sophie telling them stories of Disciples deserting their posts, or ignoring orders and fleeing. They usually didn't get far. These three inner circle Disciples, though, didn't seem in a hurry to go after the deserters. That probably meant they had given the order to leave.

One of the three Disciples was holding the reigns of a horse and was starting to climb on its back. The other two seemed to be planning to leave as well. It didn't look like there was anything for the Asters to do to scatter the Disciples. Their destruction of Mitrik's capital castle must have done the trick. The inner circle Disciples hadn't organised the camp in Mitrik's absence into some sort of army. They were leaving. They were running.

And the Asters could let them leave. But an opportunity to take down three more inner circle members of a King? And gaining even more information on Mitrik if they could? The five Asters exchanged looks, all of one mind. They couldn't pass up that chance.

"Let's go," Sky said.

The Disciple already on the horse kicked with his legs and the horse broke into action. He turned the horse down the riverbed away from the camp and followed the other fleeing Disciples.

"Send me and Sophie to him," Nathan instructed. "You three deal with the other two."

Sky had no idea what Nathan was planning to do with the Disciple on the horse. His first idea was for himself to crash down onto that Disciple himself from above. But they didn't have much time, and Nathan seemed to have a plan. Considering what he'd managed to pull off so far this mission, it didn't seem right to contradict him now.

With a wave of his hand, Sky shimmered both Nathan and Sophie off the *Angel Trail.* For a second Nathan's vision was filled with blue light. The ground under his feet gave way and he was flying through the air. The next thing he knew was the strength in his legs as he landed on the Canyon floor.

He looked around and found Sophie standing beside him. He turned his head further and found that Sky had shimmered them in between the first group of fleeing Disciples and the inner circle Disciple, who was now charging straight at them on his horse.

There was surprise on his face when Nathan and Sophie suddenly appeared on the path in front of him, but he recovered quickly. There was confusion, too; Nathan was still wearing Disciple clothes, after all. Still, after glancing at Sophie, he made no move to reach for his weapons. He seemed to make a choice not to attack Sophie and Nathan from the top of his horse as he galloped straight towards them. Instead, he barked orders at the group of Disciples behind Nathan and Sophie, who, when Nathan turned his head to look, stepped up their pace, rather than turn to fight the two Asters. The inner circle Disciple didn't command them to turn around and attack. He was letting them hurry off. But why?

Nathan didn't have time to think of an answer. He was still working out the plan he had in his head, but the horse and rider were closer than he had expected. Neither he, nor Sophie, had time to reach for their weapons before the horse was upon them. Instinctively, he and Sophie dived to the side, rolling immediately so they could jump back up to their feet.

Nathan turned and focused on his magic. His Band pulsed a bright green and he threw his arm forward. A single, thick vine appeared out of nowhere and grew at tremendous speed, flying forward and wrapping itself around the rider's upper body. The other end of the vine was in Nathan's hand. He twisted his hand so that the vine was wrapped around his wrist for extra grip. Then he pulled his arm backwards.

The Disciple was dragged off the back of his horse and crashed to the ground. Nathan tugged on the vine again, and the Disciple was pulled towards them, again with such speed. Magic soared through Nathan's body. The strength of his own arms surprised him. From the corner of his eye, he caught Sophie staring at him.

Nathan's eyes were on the Disciple now lying at their feet. The vine had wrapped itself thickly all around the Disciple's upper body, pinning his arms to the side so that he couldn't reach his weapons. Nathan stepped up to the Disciple and put one foot on the man's chest.

"Why aren't you fighting?" he asked.

The Disciple glared at Nathan, but made no move to answer him. Around them, the last group of Disciples rushed past. They cast cold glances to him and Sophie, but didn't attack. They just hurried on.

"Why leave without a fight?" Nathan asked again.

The Disciple bared his teeth at Nathan, but again said nothing.

Sophie crouched down by the Disciple. Nathan watched as she took a knife and pushed it through the side of the Disciple's neck. There was a short gurgling sound as Sophie punctured his airway, and blood streamed in. It didn't take long before the Disciple's eyes turned glassy and lifeless. Sophie stood back up and dusted herself off.

Nathan stared at her. She glanced up at him and shrugged. "He wasn't going to tell us anything."

Nathan sighed. "It was worth a try."

"Nothing?" Matu asked. He, Lian and Sky had come up beside them.

"No," Sophie replied.

Sky huffed his disappointment. He looked around. Nathan did the same. Only a few individual Disciples still hurried past the Asters, leaving the camp empty behind them. They glanced in the direction of the Asters, but did nothing more than give them a cold look. They pulled no weapons and didn't advance. It was strange; Disciples always attacked. They always wanted the glory of taking down an Aster.

So why were these Disciples acting like this? Nathan had never experienced it before. They would rather flee than stand up for what the Asters did to their King's stronghold.

All the Asters thought they would.

So why didn't they?

The entire camp was abandoned by the time the Asters searched the tents that had been left behind. Sophie had remembered where she had seen the human hikers at the riverbed, and hoped that the other group that Mitrik had planned to use in his rings would be in one of the tents near there. David Hughes seemed to have specifically dropped those fire bombs far away from where Sophie guessed they were being held. The hikers they'd already saved must have given the Affinite similar information.

None of the Asters had seen any of the Disciples take along the prisoners as they fled the camp. Sophie was glad that their destruction of the castle had been enough for these Disciples to believe Mitrik didn't have what it took to reclaim the Surface. Even though she had made that plan from terrible grief, it had still been a good plan. And it had paid off.

She wondered where Mitrik was now. Had he already heard the news of his castle being destroyed? Had he been the one to call his Disciples back, or had they fled of their own accord?

Sophie thought about Mitrik's plan, and wondered whether he'd already found the South American King. She doubted the alliance would hold now that the Asters had proven they could destroy Mitrik's capital castle from the inside.

"In here!" Lian called. He was about a hundred yards away from Sophie. He was standing in front of a tent, and ducked inside. There was a brief scream – Lian was still wearing Disciple clothes – and then Sophie heard him tell whoever was in there not to worry; he was there to rescue them.

Before they'd started searching the abandoned camp, Matu had told them how many humans they were still looking for. There had to be a Chinese man and woman, another woman with a son, a younger couple, and two professional hikers who had each been leading a group. Eight in total.

Sophie and the other Asters hurried towards Lian. Once inside the tent, they saw that Lian had already found a set of keys and was unlocking the shackles around the ankles of the humans inside. As he worked, Sophie counted them.

Eight human hikers sat huddled together against one side of the tent. Sophie let out a breath in relief. The smell of them was atrocious, but Sophie made sure she didn't make a face.

Matu and Sky helped the humans to their feet once Lian had unshackled them.

"M-m-m-my husband…" the mother stammered.

"We have him, Ma'am," Matu reassured her. "He's safe."

As if on cue, the air filled with the rattling sound of a helicopter. Sophie leant outside of the tent to look, and shielded her eyes from the flying sand whipped up by the rotor blades of the helicopter. When the blades eventually stopped moving, Sophie opened her eyes. She brushed the sand off her jacket and stepped out of the tent completely. Nathan was on her heels.

Sophie recognised David Hughes' sons first. They had been sitting in the back and were the first to jump out. David Hughes – who had been flying the helicopter – and a woman Sophie assumed was his wife, Linda, stepped out of either side of the cockpit.

"Seems like you didn't need our help out here after all," David said as he stepped towards them.

"What do you mean?" Matu asked.

"Well, they were already running off when we arrived. Axel gave us the go-ahead to help scatter the camp, but when we came here, half the camp was already leaving. So, what did you do to make them all bolt like that? Must've been something spectacular if the news reached all the way out here. Must've been... Did you kill the King? Something like that would certainly set them running, that's for sure," the Affinite rambled.

"No, we didn't kill him," Sophie said.

"We destroyed the white castle," Sky said.

"HA! That would've done it." David laughed out loud. "That must have been a sight to see, a sight indeed. Still, I am surprised they ran off like that. There were still a few inner circle Disciples bossing everyone around here, from what I could see from the air. But, good on you all, very impressive indeed."

Sophie inclined her head. "Thank you."

Behind her and Nathan, the tent flap opened and Lian stepped out. David's grin broadened as he saw Lian. "Good to see you made it out! Alive and well, I see, very good, very good." He gestured to Nathan and Matu. "Those two were worried, they were. Extremely angry that they had the magic to save you when you'd already run off to find Sophie. In a real state they were. Good thing they found ya, wasn't it? Or did you find Sophie?"

"I—well..." Lian started.

"Honey," Linda Hughes interrupted. "We really need to get a move on with these humans. They've been through enough."

David looked over his shoulder to his wife. "You're right, of course." He gestured to one of his sons. Sophie and Nathan moved aside as David and Wesley stepped towards the hikers. They started talking in hushes tones, telling their families were all right and that they would be taken to them. The hikers followed the two Affinites to the helicopter.

"Here, I thought some of you might like this," Linda said. She reached into the shoulder bag she was carrying and pulled out two bottles of water. Both Sophie and Sky accepted one gratefully.

"How does he have a helicopter?" Sky asked in between large gulps.

Jason, the Hughes' eldest son, laughed. "He's the head of the organisation that tracks down missing hikers. The job comes with its perks."

Lian came up beside them. "You get to fly along often?"

"Every now and again," Jason replied. Then he grinned, his eyes sparkling. "Never got to set anything on fire like that before, though."

"Even though it wasn't necessary anymore?" Sophie said, her mouth twitching into a smile.

Jason shrugged. "Good target practise for next time."

They laughed for a moment as they watched the hikers get strapped into the seats of the helicopter. There were exactly eight seats in the back, four across from each other, and two seats up front for the pilot and co-pilot.

David walked away from the helicopter. He turned to his sons first. "You two get started cleaning up this mess. I'll come back with back-up while your mother works on the hikers' memories."

"We can help," Sophie offered.

David turned to her and smiled. "You have done your job, Miss. Now let us do ours. We'll clean this all up. Besides, I've already rung Axel on your behalf, and he wants you back on Saluverus, A.S.A.P."

"That's fast. Do you know why?" Matu asked.

David shook his head. "Probably not for me to know, if he didn't tell me."

"Are you sure you don't need any help?" Sophie asked, looking around at the abandoned Disciple camp. About a quarter of the tents were still there, including the half-burnt down circus tent.

"It's fine, really. We've managed to keep this part of the Canyon free from other hikers or any other human onlookers. It won't take long before we've cleared it up and we can open up the trails in this section of the Canyon. Though, I don't think the *Angel Trail* will open any time soon. Those Disciples made a real job of that one, didn't they?" David laughed. The Asters had trouble laughing with him. Nathan and Matu had already told part of the story of how Nathan had managed to make a makeshift staircase to facilitate their escape. Sophie was sure that the experience was too recent to laugh about just yet.

David held out a hand and shook the hands of each of the Asters. Linda, Jason and Wesley did the same. When finished, the two sons said their goodbyes and headed off into what remained of the Disciple camp. David turned back to the helicopter, leaving only Linda standing in front of them.

"Have a safe journey back," she said. "You don't have to worry, really. This is what we do. We will let Axel know if we need any help."

Sky turned to Sophie. "Maybe they'll send your boyfriend in, like in Indonesia. Make him feel like he's doing something important."

Sophie instinctively slapped him on the shoulder. "Shut up, you idiot."

Linda thanked the Asters once more, and said goodbye another two times before turning around and walking over to the helicopter. David had already closed the side doors and Linda jumped in beside him in the cockpit.

Sophie and her brothers watched as the rotor blades of the helicopter started to slowly turn round and round. They turned away and shielded their eyes from all the sand that lifted and flew around as the helicopter rose into the air and up and out of the Canyon.

When the sand finally settled again, Matu said, "Come on, let's go home."

They stood in a circle, each holding on to the two people next to them. Sky's Band glowed blue and they all shimmered away from the Disciple camp and the Grand Canyon, and back to Saluverus.

Chapter 15

When the blue light from Sky's shimmer vanished from Lian's vision, they found themselves on the grassy courtyard at the foot of Saluverus' castle. News must have travelled fast from David Hughes to the island, because their friends were waiting for them. The twins, Asmae and Marwa, stood next to Marlena. On Marlena's other side stood Ashu and Kemal, and behind her were Arthur and Jacob.

Lian had barely blinked the blue dots from his vision before it was filled once again, but this time with a mass of messy brown hair. The moment they'd arrived, Anna threw herself at him and hugged him tightly. Lian only just managed to keep his footing as, for the second time that day, a girl had launched herself at him. When Anna finally unwound her arms from his neck and stepped back, she punched him in the shoulder.

"Ow!" Lian gasped. "What was that for?"

Anna's eyes sparkled with mischief. "Maybe don't try to die next time, okay?"

"Try? You think I was trying to die?" Lian said, clapping hands with Ashu and Kemal, who had come up beside Anna.

"Well, Arthur said you almost did." Behind Anna, Sophie had just hugged Jacob, and was talking to him and Arthur, while Sky and Matu were talking to Marwa and Asmae.

"Arthur—how would he even know that?"

"He overheard Jackson talking to Axel. So, it's true?" Anna said.

Lian shrugged. "It happens. But I'm alive, aren't I?"

Anna grinned. "Yeah. You better stay that way, okay?"

"Okay."

Anna nodded and gave him one last hug before heading off to Sophie. Arthur and Sophie were talking in hushed voices. Jacob stood beside Sophie, holding her hand and listening to the conversation. From the look on Arthur's face, he and Sophie weren't discussing anything pleasant. It didn't take a genius to figure out that Sophie had asked about Jillian and her father. Lian could tell from their body language and expressions that the news was not great.

Lian joined Sky, who was talking to Ashu now, while Matu was chatting away about bringing down Mitrik's white castle with Nathan's vines, to Kemal and Marlena. When Lian approached Sky and Ashu, the Affinite took one look at Lian and wrinkled his nose.

"You look horrible," Ashu remarked.

Lian was taken aback. He didn't have any major cuts or bruises on his face or arms. If anything, he looked more like himself than any of the others, since he had been healed right before the destruction of Mitrik's castle.

"Don't look so offended, mate." Sky laughed. "He's talking about the armour you're wearing. Disciple stuff, it really doesn't suit you."

"You might want to change, or people here might think they need to kill you," Ashu said in a low voice, a grin on his face. "Though, you still look better than Sky over here. At least you're not covered in blood. You believe he almost shook my hand?"

Lian chuckled. He hadn't had the time to ask why Sky's face and hands were completely covered in blood. It had dried now, and started peeling off his skin. It still looked horrible.

"You're here," came a voice from above. Everyone looked up. On the balcony stood Sylvia Allen. "You're expected in the Board Room." She stepped away from the balcony and vanished out of view.

"Duty calls," Matu said.

"*Boring*," Sky muttered.

Sophie whispered something to Arthur and Anna, before kissing Jacob once and heading for the stone staircase to the side of the courtyard.

Sky purposefully patted Ashu on the back, who attempted to flinch away, but not quickly enough. Some of the dried blood came loose from Sky's hand and stuck to Ashu's coat. Sky laughed before following Sophie up the stairs.

"Come get a drink later?" Ashu called after the five Asters.

"When we're off duty," Matu replied.

"When will that be?" Kemal asked.

Before Matu could open his mouth again, Sky patted him on the shoulder, sending more bits of dried blood flying. "We'll be there," he told Kemal.

The Affinites from Turkey and Ethiopia grinned and headed down the courtyard with Arthur and the twins. Marlena turned in the direction of the Medical Bay, while Anna and Jacob followed the Asters up the stone stairs and into the castle. Inside, they took a right turn towards their own rooms, while the Asters turned left to go to the Board Room.

"We can't have a drink while we're on duty," Matu was pointing out to Sky as they walked down the corridor.

"Yes, we can," Sky said. He was whistling along quite happily.

"No, we can't."

"Okay, maybe *you* can't. You get tipsy after just one beer. Us normal people on the other hand..."

"Let's just be clear that you are the only one here who would drink when you could be called out into the field, brother," Lian mentioned.

"That's because my brain still functions perfectly after a drink." Sky tapped his right temple with his finger.

"There is so much scientific research proving how wrong that statement is," Sophie remarked.

"I pride myself in being the exception to the rule."

Lian shook his head. "The things you are proud of, brother..."

Beside him, Nathan chuckled.

"You know what? Never mind. We're having that drink because we're not going to be on duty for long," Sky said.

"And how do you know that?" Matu asked.

"Are you kidding? We blew up Mitrik's castle! We scattered the camp that would lead the uprising! No King is going to attempt to retake the Surface any time soon, I am sure of it! We'll be out in no time."

"Well, here's our chance to find out," Sophie said.

They had reached the Board Room. Matu opened the door and the five Asters filed in, taking their seats at the table in the middle of the room. Axel was standing at the head of the table, carefully watching each Aster as they took their seats. Nicholas Nelson and Felix Hauser were leaning against the low cupboard underneath the large window overlooking the island. Jackson was sitting at the corner desk and, next to him, Sylvia was leaning against it.

When all the Asters had sat down, Axel looked over at Sylvia. Something unspoken was conveyed in that look, and Sylvia nodded and left the room.

As the door closed behind her, Axel turned to the Asters. "I want to congratulate you. You have successfully saved the captured human hikers and quelled the uprising of the South American King."

The Ambassador spoke very matter-of-factly. He had a stern look on his face. He didn't seem overly appreciative. There was something that wasn't being said. Even the cold and serious Ambassador was usually happier and more excited than this when the Asters came back from a successful mission. But for some reason it now seemed like he was just listing facts.

"Linda Hughes is working on the humans' memory and David's team is currently clearing the Canyon floor of what remains of the Disciple camp," he continued. "The entrance to the Underworld, which you barred up, Nathan, is still closed. The Disciples never managed to break through it. It will remain closed for the foreseeable future."

Lian noticed Sophie looking thoughtfully at Nathan, worry in her eyes. The strength that must've gone into sealing that door to such an extent that in all the time they were in the Underworld, the Disciples still hadn't managed to break through it, was a strength that Nathan had never shown before. Lian wondered if Sophie was worried about why Nathan's magic was suddenly growing stronger.

Axel Reed didn't seem to think Nathan's sudden growth in strength was anything significant. Or it wasn't the most important thing on his mind right now. He continued without mentioning it again.

"It was true that Mitrik had left the North American Underworld. We do believe an alliance with the South American King was his original plan. That plan seems to have failed. There was a short moment that we could detect Mitrik's essence in South America, but it vanished soon after. We believe that when you brought down his castle, he returned to North America and retreated further into the Underworld to a different district, calling his Disciples along with him."

"Do you know where he is now?" Matu asked.

Axel's eyes rested on Matu for a long moment before answering. "We do not. We cannot detect his essence either in South or North America. But he is a strategist. We can confidently assume he has retreated to one of his other castles and is staying behind a veil, through which we cannot track him." Axel paused for a moment. "You five did well. We won't expect him to make a move any time soon, or attempt to create another alliance either."

It was about the highest praise they could receive from Saluverus' Ambassador. By the way Axel spoke, they all knew they wouldn't get any more.

"What about Agatha Jones?" Nathan asked.

Behind Axel, Felix cleared his throat. "We have not heard anything from the Indigo. Before you ran into her, we had no idea she was so close to a King. We believe, because of your escape, Mitrik will be looking at his ranks very closely. There is a good chance we will not hear from Agatha for a long time. She will have to prove her loyalty once again, and cannot risk sending out information until she is sure she is no longer being watched," the Spymaster explained.

"But she's alive?" Sophie asked.

"We don't know that either. But believe you me, it will take a lot more than a stronghold collapsing and a King's distrust, to kill her," Felix said.

Lian let out a low whistle. He remembered the electric wave she created in the marble path. Though it had almost caused them all to fall to their deaths when the whole thing started to fall apart, it was one of the most brilliant things Lian had ever seen. If she could prove that she had nothing to do with the Asters escaping, Mitrik would certainly keep her in his ranks. Lian hadn't actually met Mitrik himself, but from how Sophie and Sky described him, the King would be too proud to throw away what he thought was the first ever Disciple Indigo.

"So, what? We just wait? She saved our lives! She's the only reason me and Sky got out of that prison cell," Sophie said.

Sky paid attention at that. "What did she have to do with that?"

Sophie looked at her brother. "She purposefully had that conversation with Mitrik's Second in front of us, so we knew Mitrik wasn't in North America. And I can bet you anything that she was the one who left the key."

Sky thought for a moment. Then he nodded slightly in understanding and said, "Huh, didn't think about that; I guess you're right. I suppose I can share the credit with her on that one."

Sophie fake-glared at her brother. "You suppose so, do you? It's not like without my plan you'd still be there now, with a bruised shoulder trying to bust the door open or anything."

Lian sniggered, while Nathan and Matu were having a hard time keeping their chuckles to themselves.

"Hey, just because using force wasn't *your* plan, doesn't mean it was a bad plan," Sky countered.

"By all accounts, it really was," Sophie replied. "But that's not the point. Is there any way to find out if Agatha's all right? We're only here because of her!"

"Agatha Jones isn't like any other Merger. She sends a signal every now and again to Glacialis to let us know that she's still alive—" Felix started.

"Glacialis?" Sophie interrupted.

Felix sighed. "She was born there; grew up there. She reports to Glacialis' Ambassador, Millie Hastings. She is the only Merger that does; every other Merger reports to me. She doesn't work the way I'd like my Mergers to work, but when she sends back information, it is of more significance than what any other Merger tells us about North America."

"She was incredible," Sky admitted.

"She is. I am glad you got to meet her," Felix said. "There is a chance you may never see her again. A woman like Agatha is married to her work in the strongest sense of the word. She will probably be in the Underworld until the day she dies."

Lian let out another low whistle.

Axel cleared his throat. He looked slightly irritable. "We will be going through every step of your mission later this week. For now, I quickly want to run through everything else you need to know. Rose, Katherine and their Bone Recovery team found nothing. We believe they were sent on a wild goose chase. We called them back, and have accepted that Cara and Tomas' remains will never be found."

The Asters were quiet, absorbing the significance of this news. It meant the line of Aster magic that Cara and Tomas possessed ended with them. No more magic of Endurance, and no more magic of Mind. Never again. It was sad and sobering knowledge. No wonder Axel's appreciation of their success was so muted.

"As for what happened to the Affinites in the Amazon, we can conclude that they were ambushed by Disciples on orders from the South American King. He has proven to be a very strategic and intelligent King. Until Percy Kelly has recovered, we will not know how those Disciples managed to surprise some of the best women and men this island has ever seen." Axel looked at every Aster at the table, but his eyes rested slightly longer on Matu. "As for Percy Kelly..." he continued slightly absently. "He has been moved to a secure location up in the cliffs for better recovery. Bianka checks up on him daily, as does Olga Masalis and speech therapist Arnar Jakobsson, to work on his speech and trauma symptoms. Hopefully, he will recover and regain a stable state of mind so that he might tell us something, anything, about the South American King." He broke off to look at each Aster in turn. "None of you are to visit him."

The Board Room was silent for a while. All the excitement and adrenaline that had been pulsing through each of the Asters during the aftermath of their mission had seeped away.

After some time, Sophie asked quietly, "Is anyone other than medical staff allowed to see him?"

Jackson answered, "Jillian, Arthur and I visit him. We are who Percy knows best. He is mostly calm when we are around."

"Do you think he will ever recover?" Matu asked.

Jackson turned to him. "It's too soon to tell, but it doesn't look good."

A silence filled the room again. Percy Jackson was a legendary soldier. Lian had heard many stories of the Icelandic twin soldiers. It was hard to imagine one being broken down to nothing. It was almost more cruel than death.

Axel was the one to break the silence. "Until Percy can give us any further information on South America, we will not send anybody else in there. We have to accept that Tomas and Cara are gone. And that Gayle... is gone. There will be no Transfers of magic, and no new Aster births. From here on out you will be the five, and only five, Asters."

Lian heard Nathan suck in a breath beside him.

Again, Axel looked at every Aster individually. "For now, you are off duty. Though, there is one more thing that you all need to know."

The Ambassador cast his eyes down to the table. There was something on his face that Lian had never seen before. Sadness? Lian had never known the Ambassador to show that sort of emotion. Nothing except for frustration or anger or annoyance. Usually directed at Sky.

The Asters waited for anybody in the room to say something. But no words ever came. Then a few moments later, the Board Room door opened, and Sylvia Allen stepped in, followed by a woman they all recognised to be Matu's mother.

Chapter 16

After cleaning themselves up and grabbing a quick bite from the dining hall, the Asters sat silently in the common room. Sophie and Sky sat on one of the sofas. Nathan was in an armchair, while Lian was sitting on the floor, leaning with his back against the brick of the fireplace. Matu was still with his mother.

Nathan had never known his father, but the thought of losing his mother... Especially after such an emotionally exhausting mission, where the loss of one of their own had seemed imminent on multiple occasions, this wasn't something any of them wanted to come home to.

Nathan hadn't felt the emotional stress of the mission at the time, but the second they'd returned and that cold curtain dropped away, he felt immensely tired. He admired how his siblings dealt with that emotion while out in the field. How they could keep their focus while their emotions were running high, was something Nathan might never understand. He worked differently that way. He didn't know why, or how. But a part of him was glad he did.

He'd seen the panic in Matu's eyes when time was running out to save Lian, and the fear in Sophie's eyes when they were facing off against Kali, before they knew she was Agatha Jones. Nathan was glad he could keep razor sharp and not be distracted by the direness of a situation.

"I can't believe it," Sophie whispered. She rubbed her hands over her face.

Sky sighed. "I just don't understand how it could've happened." He held up his hands as he added, "I mean Di-a-llo Ma-da-ki."

"He always seemed invincible," Nathan whispered.

"Then how the hell did they do it?" Lian wondered.

"Bloody snake bite at the wrong time," Sophie muttered.

"How the hell is that possible?" Sky snapped.

Sophie closed her eyes. "Happens more often than you think. It's actually not that uncommon."

"Well, it should be," Sky muttered. "I mean, what is up with that continent? Bad luck seems to follow everywhere Affinites and Asters go."

"We got the Affinites out just fine," Nathan pointed out quietly.

"It was never the King's intention to make that difficult. He delayed us just enough," Lian answered.

"Then what is it? Is it that King's genius or just pure bad luck?" Sky said.

"There's no real point in speculating," Sophie said absently. "Doesn't make Matu's dad any less gone..."

A long silence followed.

"Maybe we should go see him," Nathan offered after a while.

Sky shook his head. "Not all of us."

"I'll go," Lian said.

"Are you sure?" Sophie asked.

"Yeah," Lian replied, getting up. "I've been where he is. I know what it's like."

Sophie nodded and Sky murmured something under his breath. Without another word, Lian left the room. The door closed behind him.

Sky let out a long breath. "What are we supposed to do now? Just sit here?"

Nathan could detect the frustration in Sky's voice. Nathan didn't blame him. He knew this was how his brother dealt with pain, emotional or otherwise.

Across from him, Sophie sighed and looked up. Nathan followed her gaze. Above her was the balcony that led to Sky and Matu's rooms. There was a third bedroom up there as well. Sophie shook her head. Nathan knew what was on her mind; on who would have, maybe even should have, filled that room.

Frustration was boiling up somewhere deep within him as well, but he was too exhausted to do anything about it.

Sophie glanced up at the door of the third, empty bedroom once more, and said, "I know something we need to do. Come on."

Sophie led Nathan and Sky along the stone walkways cut into the western side of the cliffs. They walked in silence. Sophie dug her hands further into the pockets of her winter coat as the wind whipped around them. The weak sun hung low above the horizon when the three of them arrived at the Mendosa family crypt.

The two lanterns on either side of the crypt's entrance flared up as they stepped inside. The crypt was large enough for the three of them to stand side by side.

Sophie looked down at the floor where it met the back wall. It seemed like a lifetime ago that she was kneeling here, in front of a map of Brazil, and cutting her hand open again and again, trying to track a girl who couldn't be found, with her blood and magic spells. Sophie moved her thumb along the thick scars on her left palm. Those scars were there to serve as a reminder. A reminder that she was alive, and that she would fight to stay alive. That she would avenge the girl who should have lived. Who should have come here and grown strong. And ruled over them all.

Who shouldn't have died alone and afraid.

Sophie stared at the three newly engraved plaques on the wall. Behind each of them, within the wall, would be a case of glass. But there were no ashes within them. They may never know exactly what happened to the two Ceders and their future Queen. How they died. If they suffered. It all seemed so unfair.

"Here," Nathan said quietly. He was carrying a bouquet of roses he'd grown himself, and offered a single rose to Sophie. She took the rose and placed it on the ground, below the three plaques.

"May you be free," Sophie said quietly, starting the lines recited at every Affinite and Aster funeral.

Nathan handed a rose to Sky, who did the same thing. He knelt down and placed the rose next to Sophie's.

"May you feel no pain," Sky said.

"May you find peace," Nathan whispered, as he placed the third rose on the floor.

It was Sophie's turn again.

"May your deaths not be in vain."

A moment of silence, and then Sky's voice echoed through the crypt.

"You will be avenged."

Sophie cast a sideways glance at her brother. She could see the anger in his eyes as he looked at the names on the wall. Sophie knew he believed there was more that could've been done. And maybe there was. Sky, maybe even more than herself, had secretly been looking forward to Gayle's arrival.

Something new.

A challenge.

With the adrenaline from the mission gone, the anger had returned. Sophie wondered how long that would stay with him before he'd manage to let it go. There was nothing more they could do.

You will be avenged.

The final words echoed in Sophie's mind. She looked at the names on the walls. Two Asters, who became Ceders, had lived—truly lived. And a young Queen who never knew who she was until it was too late.

Such an injustice.

But they wouldn't die in vain. The Asters would make sure those final words would come true. Whether it was tomorrow, or next week, or next year. They would face the South American King, and the Asters would have their justice.

"You will be avenged," Sophie whispered again.

The three Asters left the crypt. Instead of heading back through the cliff tunnels to the castle, they remained on the walkway. Sophie stood in between Nathan and Sky as they looked out over the Norwegian Sea. Sky was leaning on the stone balcony with his forearms. The sun was hovering just above the horizon, sending streaks of gold and orange across the darkened water.

"So..." Sophie said. "It's just us now."

"Yep," Sky murmured.

"Just us," Nathan said softly.

Sophie placed her hand on Sky's arm while resting her head against Nathan's shoulder. They were quiet a little longer. The sun touched the top of the water as twilight descended all around them. The wind had died down; they were surrounded by complete silence.

A while later, footsteps sounded on the stone steps to their left. The three Asters all turned their heads and found Lian and Matu walking up to them.

Sophie's heart broke at the sight of her oldest brother. He appeared so worn and beaten down. Used to his height and size, Sophie couldn't bear seeing him look so small. And yet here he was, weak and broken. North America had been a rollercoaster and a half, in terms of emotion and energy. How do you come back from that, only to find out when you got home that you'd lost your father?

"Hey," Sophie said, greeting them both.

"Hey," Lian answered softly.

The three of them watched Matu, waiting for what their brother wanted them to do, or say.

"Don't ask me how I'm doing. Just... don't," he said.

Nathan nodded silently.

"All right," Sophie replied softly.

Matu and Lian stepped towards them.

"You left a note saying you were laying roses by Gayle's crypt," Matu said.

Nathan looked up. "Do you want to?"

Matu nodded.

Silently, Nathan led both Matu and Lian into the crypt behind them. Sophie turned her head to watch them go. When she was sure they were out of earshot, she turned to Sky.

"I'm worried, Sky," she said.

Sky turned to her. "About Matu?"

Sophie shook her head. "Nathan."

Sky looked over his shoulder to where they could both now hear the whispers of the words of Aster and Affinite funerals.

"Please tell me you've noticed," Sophie whispered. "The way they described him saving Lian. The strength of his vines; his strength in general. It's not normal."

"I have noticed."

"He turned eighteen six months ago, Sky. His powers stopped growing at least six months before that. It makes no sense that they're growing again. It's not natural."

"Maybe he didn't know he could do it. Maybe he's been able to do this for a year, but he's never had to, so he never knew," Sky offered.

"Do you really believe that?"

Sky thought for a moment. "No. He would've put more effort into trying to beat me at trainings." Sky offered her a smile, but it faltered.

Sophie let out a sigh. "I don't want to be worried."

"You would be worried even if you don't need to be."

Sophie glanced sideways at her brother. "Something might be wrong."

"Or something might not be," Sky countered. "He is stronger. You'd be blind not to notice. But it's not necessarily a bad thing. Maybe it's that thing they say about blind people—how they have a stronger sense of smell?"

Sophie couldn't help but chuckle at that. "*Smell?* Of all the senses you could have chosen, you went with *smell?*"

Sky smiled. "I'm just saying. Maybe the stars are compensating. Maybe that's what's happening to Nathan; it only started since the Queen died. Maybe it will happen to all of us."

Sophie gave it some thought. Despite his strange analogy, Sky might actually be on to something. Or Sophie just hoped he was. *Magic has a way of keeping itself strong*; that's what they said. It's why usually when two Asters fell in love, twins were born, each child possessing one of the parents' powers.

"We're going to face something stronger and more powerful than any of our ancestors have. That's why Gayle was born the way she was. Maybe Nathan's powers growing isn't the worst thing in the world.

Maybe don't overthink it just yet," Sky said.

"But we still watch him," Sophie countered. Footsteps from behind told her Matu, Nathan and Lian were coming back outside. She added with a whisper, "We make sure it's not getting out of control."

All Sky did was give her a short nod, for Matu, Nathan and Lian had re-joined them by the stone balcony.

For a moment the five of them looked out over the Sea. Sophie wasn't quite sure what to say. She didn't know if Matu wanted them to say anything. They couldn't just start any conversation on any topic like any other time. The news was too raw, their senses too exposed.

Thankfully, Matu seemed to think talking about anything random *was* a good idea. Though what he asked, wasn't the easiest thing to respond to.

"What were you guys talking about?" he asked.

Sophie and Sky exchanged an awkward glance. Sophie's head immediately filled with possible random topics she could mention, but it was Sky who answered.

"The impending threat that Gayle's birth predicted that we're some day going to have to fight on our own," he said in the most casual of tones Sophie had ever heard. Everyone stared at Sky, Lian even open-mouthed. Sophie closed her eyes and forced herself not to slap her brother for saying something so stupid. Of all the things Sky could have said, why, in such a sad moment, tell the truth?

Then, to everyone's surprise, Matu snorted. "That's not exactly a happier subject, now is it?"

Sky shrugged. "You asked."

Matu actually chuckled, and leaned down on the stone wall with his elbows, shaking his head.

"I do wonder what will happen," Lian said quietly. "That King has blown up everything we thought our future would be. None of that's left now."

169

"I believe we'll survive it," Sophie said resolutely. "I know I can't start talking about believing how everything happens for a reason. I used to believe that, but dammit, what reason can possibly justify everything that has happened? Everything that's gone..."

Sophie glanced at Matu. He looked at her with such sadness in his eyes.

"We just have to keep fighting," she continued in a determined voice. She didn't want the sadness to envelop her. Not again. "We will face whatever comes. We faced a *King* this week. *And we survived.* Even when we were split up and operating apart. We've proven we can handle it. Sure, we had some help, but we know more for next time. We'll be even smarter and even stronger. I believe that. I believe the five of us, all of us together, will be enough. We will find a way to be enough."

She looked at her brothers. They were all looking at her. There was something more she wanted to say. It might be too much, or it might be just what the situation needed.

"You know, the King took away our Queen. He burnt away our future. But we rose," Sophie added. She straightened her back and stared out into the distance. "*Just like a phoenix we rose from the ashes.*"

Sky snorted. The others chuckled. Even Matu.

"*What?*" Lian asked, half laughing.

"You've lost us," Sky added.

Sophie hoped she'd get this reaction, so she played along. She frowned. "It's a mythological bird that dies in a fire and is reborn from its ashes continuously," she explained.

The boys all stared at her.

Sophie rolled her eyes. "You know what, *never mind*. I thought it was a nice analogy, that's all."

Even though Matu was leaning down, still looking out over the Sea, Sophie caught a twitch of his lips as he tried to keep himself from smiling.

"*Riiiight,*" Sky drawled.

Sophie slapped his shoulder. "Oh, shut up. I like the analogy."

"That makes one of us," Sky replied.

Sophie glared up at him, but her eyes were far from angry. Her mouth wobbled as they looked at each other.

Their short moment of fun died away quickly, but the sadness had ebbed away slightly. Sophie knew that would come and go in waves. One simple joke wasn't going to fix it. She just wanted to remind Matu that his siblings would always be his siblings. That they would always be there to make him feel better, even when the whole world seemed to be crashing down around him.

Sophie looked along the walkway at all her brothers, and thought about what they had survived; what they had achieved, together. They had saved captured humans, brought the capital castle of a King crashing down, and broken apart an uprising to reclaim the Surface of the earth.

That was far from nothing.

Sophie smiled to herself. The five of them against the world. It didn't seem so scary. Sophie would charge straight into hell for the people on this walkway, and she knew they would do the same for her. Whatever they would face, and they all knew they would come to face something utterly terrifying, and horrid, and challenging, and deadly, eventually, they would face it together.

Just them.

A sort of calm descended upon them.

They'd made their peace with it. With whatever may come. They would welcome it. And they would face it with all guns blazing.

Epilogue

With night setting in over the island, the shack darkened as well. Percy Kelly made no move to turn on a light. He let the darkness settle around him. He liked it better that way. He was left alone in the night.

Every day they would come. The Greek psychotherapist and the Icelandic speech therapist. Percy recognised them. Vaguely remembered their names. But as soon as a name came to him, it vanished again somewhere in to the recesses of his mind where he couldn't reach it.

It was that way with almost everything now. Nothing he wanted to do, or say, or think, stayed with him long enough for him to do anything with it. His mind was fractured. All the pieces floating around in the darkness.

He recognised his daughter. She visited him every now and again. She looked as broken as Percy felt. What had her life become... Percy couldn't do anything about it. He had no control over his body anymore.

He'd lost the control since that one day.

That day he'd found Eva.

That day he'd seen how she died.

How she was killed.

How she was slaughtered.

The eyes of her killer stayed with him. Haunted him in his dreams. He saw them every time he closed his eyes.

The pure hatred he'd seen there. And then joy at his disgust, at his horror, as he watched. There was nothing he could do as he watched.

That was all he saw now.

Eva's butchery and those eyes, those savage green eyes.

And every time either of those stupid therapists came in, they magnified those visions; those memories.

And he'd lose control.

He wanted to tell them so badly. He wanted to say what he'd seen, what they needed to look out for, when more and more Affinites were sent in to find out what happened. Percy prayed no one would ever be sent in again.

But he couldn't tell them.

No words came out. At least, not ones they could understand. Percy couldn't form a single sentence. He couldn't even give them a hint; any indication at what he'd seen.

His body reacted for him. Despite him.

There was a spell, for an Aster to see his memories.

If only he could let magic come close.

But he'd vowed to himself, no magic would ever come near him again. He would never let it touch his skin again. If he never saw one glowing wrist again, it'd be too soon.

If only he could tell them.

He wanted to tell them so badly.

They needed to know.

They needed to know they weren't dealing with the South American King.

At least not only with him.

Percy shouted out in frustration.

They needed to know.

Since Gayle's death, South America had become not only dangerous, but treacherous and lethal.

Because she wasn't dead.

She was alive.

She was evil.

THE END

Acknowledgements

Firstly, I want to thank my incredible dream team:

    Tina, for standing by me every step of the way from day one.

    Carlota, for always being there to be my sounding board.

    Timothy, for your everlasting energy and insights.

    Peggy, for your brilliant eye for detail.

    And a brilliant thank you to the newest member of this dream team: Aster! What a hilarious coincidence that your name is the same as my series. Your unique perspective and – let's face it, sometimes – just common sense, have improved my writing beyond what I thought possible.

Secondly, a thank you to my awe-inspiring parents. You are my heroes and I would have never made it this far without either of you.

Thirdly, let me thank my ridiculously talented designer, Arjuna Jay, who makes bringing my vision to life seem so easy. You can reach Arjuna at arjunajayofficial.artstation.com.

Finally, I am so grateful to a few more people who knew I would make it to this day:

    Nick, any time I veered off course, I remembered you telling me how at heart I was an author. Those words never failed to help me find my way back.

    Rob, every time you saw me you told me again of that empty space on your bookshelf where you would put my first novel. Now you can finally fill it.

Juliette, you gave me such brilliant insights that improved my storytelling tremendously.

Sanne, you helped to keep me believing in my stories and what they could become, as long as I didn't give up.

Marissa, you were there at the beginning. I don't think either of us thought that those original, silly ideas would ever turn into anything. But, oh my, look at what they have become.

From the Author

Thank you for reading *A Threat To Remain.* If you loved the book I would really appreciate it if you would take a moment to write a short review, as it will really help new readers find my books.

If you'd like to be kept informed about the progress of other books in the Aster series, free extra content, and more, visit my website francesellenbooks.com and sign up to my email list, or follow me on instagram.com/francesellen__/.

All the books in the Aster Prequel Novella series

A Queen To Come

A World To Lose

A Threat To Remain

From The Ashes

In this first of six books in the Aster Original Series, publishing in 2022, we meet up with the Asters, one year on from the end of *A Threat To Remain*.

The South American King seems to be hatching a new... a different plan, in his attempt to rise up and take the Surface for himself.

One year later, the Asters have trained harder, have got smarter. They are fiercely determined to be one step ahead of the King who killed their Queen. And to avenge her death once and for all.

But there are hidden truths that are about to be revealed; truths about the night Gayle Mendosa died, and the day the Asters brought down the North American King.

Avenging the young Queen a year after her death may not be as straightforward as the five Asters hoped. Especially when a third party, who seems to be neither on the Asters' side, nor that of their enemy's, starts getting involved.

Join Matu, Sky, Sophie, Nathan and Lian, as their bond, magic, resilience and strength gets tested to the limit in the first full-length Aster novel.